"I did." And it wa

"Yeah. Makes us better people, huh?" That drawl was so deep. Like slow-running molasses.

"That's the rumor. Makes things a little easier."

"Like lube."

He blinked. Click. "Yes, exactly. Emotional lube."

Don't laugh. Don't laugh.

Noah snorted, this truly rip-roaring sound, and they were off again, laughing just like they had in the truck in Grand Junction. He was leaning against Noah, almost howling with pure joy.

God, it felt good to let go and just wail with laughter. He thought it had been years.

"Damn, honey. When you let yourself laugh...." Noah looked at him like he was... hell, like he was worth staring at.

The laughter faded, and his cheeks heated again. It had to be the booze and the fire. Had to. All they needed was a fuzzy rug and it was a lead-in to a porno.

Boom chicka wow wow.

Christ.

WELCOME TO
DREAMSPUN DESIRES

Dear Reader,

Love is the dream. It dazzles us, makes us stronger, and brings us to our knees. Dreamspun Desires tell stories of love featuring your favorite heartwarming heroes, captivating plots, and exotic locations. Stories that make your breath catch and your imagination soar.

In the pages of these wonderful love stories, readers can escape to a world where love conquers all, the tenderness of a first kiss sweeps you away, and your heart pounds at the sight of the one you love.

When you put it all together, you find romance in its truest form.

Love always finds a way.

Elizabeth North

Executive Director
Dreamspinner Press

BA Tortuga

FINDING MR. WRIGHT

PUBLISHED BY

Published by
DREAMSPINNER PRESS

5032 Capital Circle SW, Suite 2, PMB# 279,
Tallahassee, FL 32305-7886 USA
www.dreamspinnerpress.com

Finding Mr. Wright
© 2017 BA Tortuga.

Cover Art
© 2017 Bree Archer.
http://www.breearcher.com
Cover content is for illustrative purposes only and any person depicted on the cover is a model.

ISBN: 978-1-63533-873-7
Digital ISBN: 978-1-63533-874-4
Library of Congress Control Number: 2017904707
Published September 2017
v. 1.0

Printed in the United States of America
(∞)
This paper meets the requirements of
ANSI/NISO Z39.48-1992 (Permanence of Paper).

BA TORTUGA, Texan to the bone and an unrepentant Daddy's Girl, spends her days with her basset hounds, getting tattooed, texting her sisters, and eating Mexican food. When she's not doing that, she's writing. She spends her days off watching rodeo, knitting, and surfing Pinterest in the name of research. BA's personal saviors include her wife, Julia Talbot, her best friend, Sean Michael, and coffee. Lots of coffee. Really good coffee.

Having written everything from fist-fighting rednecks to hard-core cowboys to werewolves, BA does her damnedest to tell the stories of her heart, which was raised in Northeast Texas, but has heard the call of the high desert and lives in the Sandias. With books ranging from hard-hitting GLBT romance, to fiery ménages, to the most traditional of love stories, BA refuses to be pigeonholed by anyone but the voices in her head.

Website: www.batortuga.com
Blog: batortuga.blogspot.com
Facebook: www.facebook.com/batortuga
Twitter: @batortuga

By BA Tortuga

DREAMSPUN DESIRES
#6 – Trial by Fire
#30 – Two Cowboys and a Baby
LEANING N
#16 – Commitment Ranch
#42 – Finding Mr. Wright

Published by **DREAMSPINNER PRESS**
www.dreamspinnerpress.com

For my wife, my one and only. Love you, babe. BA

Acknowledgments

MANY thanks to Jaymi for her constant love and support.

Prologue

MID-MAY in the Roaring Fork Valley was stunning. All the wildflowers were blooming up in the high meadows around them, and down in Glenwood it was nice but not too warm to hit the Hot Springs Pool.

It was also boom time for the Leanin' N Ranch, which meant Ford Nixel spent more time on the phone with wedding planners and team builders than he did listening to clients talk about environmental law.

He chuckled at himself. No one on earth would have thought that his happy ass would be sitting here, earphone in, trying to make the big deals that kept the ranch afloat. Not him. Not for a second, but it was what he was doing, and he was over the moon about it.

"Leanin' N Ranch, this is Ford," he said into the mouthpiece.

"Mr. Ford, this is Mason O'Reilly from Rustic Romance. We worked together on the Stephens/Belen wedding?"

"Of course." He'd really enjoyed working with Mason, even if Stoney thought the man was a little… bossy.

"I'm trying to plan a rather large event for mid-June, and I was wondering if the Leanin' N had any availability."

"What are your dates?" A large event in mid-June would be great. They were surprisingly wedding bare right now.

"I'm hoping for the smack dab center. I need room for two fifty for four days and probably four or five cabins for the week before."

"Two fifty." *Holy shit.* He picked up his extra cell and texted Stoney: *Get in here.* "So, is this a wedding?"

"It is. I haven't spoken to the couple yet, but the corporation sent my assistant numbers, if you get me."

His phone mooed: *Omw*

"Right. So we can probably accommodate them all, but some lodgings might be rustic. Then again, your folks love rustic."

See him stall.

"That is my sweet spot. These guys want the whole redneck wedding—horses, mason jars, burlap, shiplap, doughnut walls. All of it. Live band at the rehearsal dinner and the wedding. I'm willing to price out other hotels if we can get shuttles."

"We absolutely can. We have a guy who has everything from buses to limos to sleighs. We also have access to yurts." He loved that word—*yurt.*

He heard the sound of Stoney's boots on the hardwood, and his own personal cowboy came zooming around the corner.

Ford held up a hand, then pointed to his notepad, which read *wedding, 250*.

His husband's eyes went huge, just wide as saucers. "No shit?" he whispered.

Ford nodded. "So, we can definitely talk turkey, Mason. You mind if I put you on speaker so Stoney can sit in?"

"Of course not. You know I live to torture your man."

"I do know that." He hit Speaker, winking at Stoney at the same time. "Okay, let's talk yurts."

"We can do all sorts of fancy-assed tents and such. They got some amazing toilet options and all. They even got showers." Ah, his classy man.

Mason chuckled warmly. "Okay, then what I'll do is send them the options and get you a firm number of overnight guests. I'll need food for the whole two fifty for the wedding, and they want just the kind of dishes your chef does, so rather than hiring a catering company, I wanted to give him the chance to hire in waitstaff and sous chefs for the event."

"We'll get you a quote by the end of the week."

"I need to give these guys an answer Thursday. Can you get me a number Wednesday?"

"I'll need the exact numbers today," Ford countered.

"I can do that. I have an inhumanly efficient assistant."

"You're such a lawyer," Stoney whispered.

Ford winked. He wheeled and dealed. That was his job. Negotiation. It had served him well with his stepson too, because ten was the age at which boys began to bargain for things. "Good deal. I'll have a proposal to you Wednesday, with some options for housing here and shuttling in guests."

"Thanks, man. You know I love working with you guys. You're my first choice. Don't let me down."

"Little butthead," Stoney mouthed.

"We got this, Mason. Thanks for the opportunity."

"Tell your husband I don't need any of the wedding party dumped into the watering trough this time."

Ford held back a bark of laughter. "You got it. I'll talk to you soon, Mason."

He hung up and sat back in his chair. "Two hundred and fifty guests, babe."

"Jesus. That's… that's a lot of folks." Stoney plopped down in a chair, staring at him. "A lot a lot."

"Mason says we can do shuttles if we have to, and he'll price out Aspen and Glenwood hotels. The bulk of it will be the wedding day, right? Food, tents for the bride and groom parties, a couple fancy portable bathrooms with sinks and all." Ford began making notes.

"We need to call Geoff in here, honey. We'll have to hire in help too."

"I know. We'll need to slam together a total budget pretty quick." Ford felt a surge of adrenaline go through him. He did love a challenge.

"Look at you, all riled up, and it's gonna be wasted on writing a proposal…."

"Oh, you know paperwork revs my engine, baby. I get all hot and bothered when I tally up the profit margins." He waggled his eyebrows at Stoney. "I'll be especially hot if you get Geoff to make pizza."

"You and your pizza." His own personal Texan stood up, walked over, and leaned down to kiss him like the world was about to end.

He slid one hand up around the back of Stoney's head to hold him in place. This was what really got Ford fired up. His husband, his kid, his ranch. Home. He loved that they were making a go of it. The kiss ended reluctantly, their lips separating with a pop.

"Mmm. Okay, that was worth a pizza. You want sausage?" Stoney waggled his eyebrows just like Ford had.

"Always." Ford winked. "You get Geoff, and I'll call Angie up so we can all plan together?"

"On it." Sure enough, his cowboy was on that phone, texting so fast his thumbs blurred.

Cowboys and cell phones. Lord.

It was like peanut butter and jelly, but with Wrangler butts. Oh, woo. What a thought.

He picked up his phone to call down to the barn office to get Angie up. The livestock manager answered with a husky laugh.

"He's already texted me, boss."

"Oh man. He's so fast. Is Tanner down there?"

"He's got Quartz in the stalls mucking."

"Oh, good deal. Okay. See you in a few." Ford hung up with Angie and opened his laptop so he could get a doc going to record this brainstorm.

He glanced at Stoney. That was the best part of his job. His life. Right there.

"They're coming, honey. You're thinking hard. What's causing that smoke pouring out of your ears?"

"Just thinking about peanut butter and jelly, baby."

Stoney raised a brow. "You're hungry?"

"Not that way. Too bad we're about to have a meeting…." He let Stoney figure that one out.

He got a look—one that said that at some point, they would be alone together and he would have a prayer meeting with his favorite cowboy.

Ford tried for angelic. He figured it came off more devilish, but one way or the other, he was going to end up getting what he needed.

Chapter One

"**MASON,** are you coming into the office today?"

Mason rolled his eyes hard enough he felt his optic nerves stretch. "Absolutely. No problem. You do have it on your calendar that I'm in fucking Denver, right, Trev?"

"OMG. This is your goddaughter's birthday party. I had that as next week!"

Did people really say OMG? Like out loud? "Why haven't I fired you yet, Trev?"

"Because no one else can put up with the hillbillies you party plan for and keep most of the deets in line." Trevor's voice dripped sarcasm.

"Right. The key word here being *most*." He grabbed a bunch of grapes, along with a watermelon for Jaycee's watermelon shark basket thing.

He'd never planned a shark-themed party before, but for that little girl? Anything.

"Hey, you keep changing your personal schedule. That is not my prob."

"What did you need, man?" He texted Rick as he talked and shopped: *Do you guys have a melon baller?*

"I need you to approve the email I sent about the Preston/Wright wedding. I had to adjust the budget to include cornholing."

God, he loved that these rich, fancy-assed people were having to add cornholing to their line items. "Sure. I'll look at it in the next twenty minutes or so. Is that Maydell lady still giving you troubles?"

"Not today. I do need to send her that quote, though. Where does one get cornhole boards made?"

"Talk to Leanin' N. They might have some, but their hand, Tanner, is a great woodworker."

The text beeped in with *Duh.*

He shot back: *I was assuming you queens weren't a cliché. Do you need anything not party-related while I'm out?*

"Okay. They want a bunch personalized, plus one just for them."

"What? A bunch of boards?"

"Yes." Trev sighed. "Are you paying attention?"

"No. I am shopping for a shark party. In Denver. This is a challenge. See what Tanner would charge."

"Will do. You'll be back Monday?"

"I'm driving home Sunday afternoon, yeah."

Jefferson needs Virgil Root Beer

Lord, Jefferson was a spoiled brat and the dearest man alive.

On it. Diet or regular?

"Okay. Well, have fun at the shark party. Tell everyone I said hi."

"Will do. They'll be up in August, for sure."

The zero

Got it

"Oh, good." Trev chuckled. "I swear to God, boss, if this lady calls me one more time…."

"I know. I know. Just remember this wedding is paying your salary for a year." The Wright Corporation was ginormous, this wedding a huge feather in his little event-planning cap.

"You know better. I'll be sweetness and light. By-eee."

He shook his head, grabbed some strawberries and, ooh, cherries. He'd pit them and put them in the shark for a little blood action.

His goddaughter was a little bloodthirsty and the light of his life.

The phone rang again, Ford Nixel's name showing up, so Mason swiped. "Hey, there. What's up?"

"Hey, man. Are you busy? I need to talk to you about the site visit this next week."

"I have time." Multitasking was his life.

"Cool. We have a big party in while the site inspection is going on. A one-day yoga retreat."

"That shouldn't be an issue at all. In fact, I may need a little savasana."

"Yes, well, I just wanted to warn you. These guys are… naked a lot."

Mason stumbled and damn near ran into an endcap of Cheez-Its. "Th-thanks for the warning."

Jesus Christ on a crutch.

"I'm sorry, Mason. I couldn't turn these guys down. Repeat clients. I can totally have someone to help you avoid pitfalls."

"Ford, I'm a healthy gay man with an appreciation for the male form. I won't run screaming. I promise." Spring wood? Maybe. It had been a while.

"Not you. Your client. I mean, who are they sending to do the walk-through? If it's the Maydell lady, we could be in deep trouble."

"I'm going to do a virtual walk-through, and then I'll schedule things with you while I'm there."

"Ah, so no one is coming up from the wedding party?"

"Apparently they're leaving everything to me. The entire wedding party will arrive the week of the ceremony."

"Wow. That's…. I hope you have a real grasp of what they want."

"You and me both, man." He didn't really have a choice, did he? No. These guys wanted a rustic, fun, high-class redneck wedding, and Mason intended to give it to them.

"Well, then I won't worry about the walk-through. I was just wanting to tell you in case the client was coming."

"I appreciate it. I'm going to come Tuesday, yeah? That's on your calendar?" He grabbed mixed nuts to spice, some tortilla chips, and…. Pace. There. Excellent.

"Yep. Stoney has it circled in red. Geoff will have a tasting for you." Ford sounded pretty relieved.

"Oh, you know Geoff is one of my favorite people on the planet." Hrm. Did he want to do super kitschy and make pizza rolls? Jaycee loved them, and her dads never let her have them.

"Any requests? You kinda left the menu up to him, save the deviled eggs."

"I want hard-core, upscale redneck. I mean, I want over-the-top." He threw the pizza rolls in the cart.

"Geoff loves a challenge." Ford chuckled now, clearly more relaxed.

"Tell him to go wild. We can brainstorm Tuesday."

"Sounds great. Thanks, man. Later." Ford clicked out, and Mason pondered pudding cups.

His job as the godfather was to spoil her in every way possible, and he took it very seriously. She loved butterscotch pudding.

So did Jefferson. Into the cart.

Swiss cake rolls for Rick and they were cooking with gas. Then he put in some M&M's. Those were for him.

He was loaded for bear. Now he just had to go carve a sharktomelon for the prettiest five-year-old on earth.

Chapter Two

MASON pulled into the Leanin' N Ranch at 10:00 a.m. Tuesday morning, already fighting the migraine from hell. There'd been a wreck in the Eisenhower Tunnel Sunday, he'd been on the road for hours, and then he'd had to run to the Junction to deal with a team-building emergency. He'd stopped in the office, left instructions with Trev, and hauled his poor, overworked Terrain back out past Aspen.

He sat for a second, just closing his eyes as he breathed, in and out, in and out.

No one bothered him, though he knew two of the hands and at least one yogi had seen him pull in. They were very live and let live at the Leanin' N. The thought made him chuckle.

Eventually, though, Stoney River tapped on the window, the cowboy's craggy face appearing, eyes like chips of emerald. "You dying, man?"

"You wish."

"Not so. You make my husband a lot of money."

"Not you?" He motioned, and Stoney stepped back to let him out. "I need coffee."

"Money isn't my problem, man. Coffee, though? That I can provide. Come on."

"Thanks." He grabbed his laptop bag before closing up the SUV. He rubbed the back of his neck with his free hand. "I don't suppose the yoga people brought in a masseuse."

"They did, in fact. Two. One pretty little boy from Carbondale and a big, hairy bear man who could break you in two from over by Vail."

"Oh, you are a flirt." Maybe he could get tag-teamed. Was that bad?

"I may be married, but I ain't dead." Those green eyes twinkled. "You iron out a menu, and I'll set you up an appointment."

"Thank you. I have a headache that's threatening to destroy me."

"You want some Tylenol?"

"If anyone has Excedrin, I'll take that." He smiled. "I'll make it."

"Come on to the kitchen. Geoff will offer some scary-assed herbal remedy, and I'll sneak you Excedrin from my medicine cabinet."

"My hero." Mason meant it too. He would be in Stoney's debt.

"That's me. Cowboy Superman." A guy walked by, stacked to the ceiling and naked as the day was long. "Namaste," Stoney called.

The guy nodded and grinned, just happy as a pig in shit.

"I assume your kiddo...."

"At his grandpa's. He's not really... ready for random nudity." Stoney's voice dropped. "I got to admit, the first time some customer walked through the kitchen nekkid, I damn near dropped my teeth."

"I bet. How's Geoff holding up?"

"Well, I had to tell him he couldn't strip off and cook. Health code violations."

"Shame." He walked into the kitchen and held his arms open. "Geoffy!"

"Oh, Mason. How are you, you crazy little man? Upscale redneck? I adore you." The little man came bebopping over and grabbed him in a tight hug that threatened to dislodge his spine and realign all his chakras. "Trev is sounding a little hysterical on the phone. Have you been into the office?"

"Does he micromanage you, Stoney?"

Stoney shot him a glance from over one shoulder. "Shit, man. I live here with him. He gets my kid to do it."

Mason chuckled. "God, it smells good. Hazelnut coffee?"

"Hazelnut and cinnamon with a hint of vanilla. Magical. You look like your head hurts. Are you okay?" Strong hands landed on his shoulders and spun him, fingers immediately digging in and kneading.

"Oh." He let his head fall forward on his neck, his tension beginning to melt away. Why wasn't Geoff his type? He could do this all day.

A cup of perfect coffee appeared before him then, and Mason was in heaven. This was why he went out of his way to use this place—the best coffee, an unbeatable view, rustic luxury, and people who actually gave a shit.

"Hey!" Angie, the head wrangler, walked in, then tugged off her cowboy hat. "I smell hazelnut. Mason, how's it hanging?"

"Hey, lady. I'm going to steal Geoff away."

Stoney handed Angie the cup of coffee he'd been making and started another one.

"No, you won't. This is where he belongs. Thanks, boss. Your better half is on his way, walking bowlegged. Good job last night."

"Angie!" Stoney's cheeks went hot pink. "Too much sharing."

"Sorry." She winked, looking wicked as hell. "This whole yoga retreat needs naked girls."

Ford walked in, all long-legged and wearing the same jeans and button-downs everyone else was and making it look like they were utterly designer. "Find a naked-girl yoga retreat that needs a home and I'm absolutely willing to do it. Hey, Mason. Coffee, baby? Please?"

Mason watched Stoney hand over another cup of coffee and grab another mug. He couldn't stop the smile on his face for anything. Well, except when Geoff grabbed his head like a chiropractor and popped his neck.

Oh God.

"Did you kill him?" Angie asked. "Because if you did, I'm totally taking pictures."

"Hey, I have never killed anyone with my ministrations," Geoff intoned.

"My headache is gone." Mason stared at Stoney, who was laughing at him.

"I told you he'd have some hippy-dippy answer." Stoney grinned, utterly unrepentant, and took a deep drink of his coffee.

"I would never let Geoff kill you, Mason." Ford sat down next to Angie, and they bumped shoulders. "Did you get the vet up for that one horse that has the hurt hoof?"

Angie nodded. "He'll be up in an hour or so. He's on rounds."

"Excellent."

The conversation flowed around Mason for a little while, a plate of banana bread and blueberry muffins appearing out of nowhere.

This place was magical.

Geoff was like a sprite or something. Fairy? Brownie? Hell if he knew. The guy was unstoppable.

"So, what can you tell us about these guys, Mason?" Geoff asked.

"Surprisingly little. The wedding's being financed by a corporation out of Texas, relatively hush-hush for a two-hundred-and-fifty-guest affair. Sam Wright and Doug Preston. I haven't even spoken to either one. They're in… Tibet climbing mountains or snorkeling with turtles or rescuing sharks or something." He didn't think either one of them worked beyond just being rich.

"Ah. Texas money." Stoney's tone was wry. "I'll walk you through the stuff we have ready. Tanner made a dozen cornhole boards, and he's waiting for you to give him details for the groom and groom's boards."

"They're doing denim and leather for their 'colors.'" He was hoping it didn't end up looking like a leather-daddy wedding. That would clash with his burlap swags.

"We can totally work with that. Do a nice faded denim and it won't look too city." Geoff shrugged when they all stared. "What? Dark denim is for people back East."

"Like in Denver?" Angie asked.

"Like New York or something. I hated that trend." Geoff scowled, but he couldn't hold the expression long.

"Faded denim I have. In yardage. Let's talk menus, Geoff. Share your thoughts with me."

"Well, you said upscale redneck Texas. I chatted with our resident Texan." Geoff jerked his head at Stoney. "We came up with everything from chicken-fried steak fingers with cream gravy dipping sauce to armadillo eggs. You said they wanted deviled eggs, so I thought some with bacon and jalapeno and some classic."

"Absolutely. I want tacos, grape-jelly meatballs, and some version of Li'l Smokies. We'll need brisket, potato salad, beans for the plate dinner, I think. Maybe a brisket-rib-turkey platter served family style?"

"Do we need a vegetarian option?"

He blinked. "Do Texans come in vegetarian?"

Stoney snorted. "Rich ones might. Or foreigners. What if they have friends from Tibet or wherever they are?"

"Hmm. Okay, what about something like black-eyed pea fritters?"

"Are you gonna make queso, Geoff?" Stoney asked.

"I'm not going to ask Geoff to make cheese, Stoney. He has a budget to work with."

Stoney blinked. "Velveeta and Ro-Tel. Costs about six bucks."

"We're having a Colorado/Texas language barrier thing. Of course we'll have queso and nachos too. Maybe taquitos." Geoff winked at Mason, who still felt like he didn't get the joke. That was probably okay, but he didn't think Stoney got it either.

"Do you have a budget workup?"

Geoff moved to his little office corner of the kitchen to open his fold-down desk. "Are you having the cakes brought in, or am I contracting those with Dina?"

Lord. Dina was a lovely, if batty, old lady who would decorate any cake Geoff baked. She made gorgeous gum-paste flowers, but this was two guys.

"I have a bakery down in Aspen that's doing the cake and the grooms' cake. You're in charge of the cupcakes in to-go boxes for everyone, the doughnuts for the doughnut wall, and whatever little sweets are needed otherwise." They'd decided on housing the wedding party at the ranch, along with about fifty of the couple's friends, but the rest were going to stay in Aspen with shuttles running them up for the ceremony and reception, thank God. "Did we arrange the portable toilets?"

"I got Fancy-Assed Porta-Potties on it."

He spun around and stared at Ford. "Those women are a nuisance!"

They were notorious for their signs around the Roaring Fork area, their swagger, and their excessive wearing of flannel.

Angie growled. "Careful, bud. They do have a shitty job."

"They'll also do two luxury portable bathrooms with sinks and showers and hookups for two weeks for six fifty," Ford said. "You can't beat their deals."

"Six fifty. Oh man. Yeah. That frees up some budget items, doesn't it?" It was expensive to get Texas wildflowers in Colorado in June. Damned expensive.

Ford looked a bit smug. "It does. Lets us get some new linens and soap baskets and shit."

"Works for me. Let's get that soap company in Santa Fe? The one that does all the rich scents that you used for the Gregory job?" Those had been magical— leather and black pepper and cinnamons. Masculine and wonderful.

"You got it." Stoney waved a hand at Geoff. "Can you make a note, man?"

"I'm on it, boss."

"Good deal. Angie, I see Doc's truck. I'm going to leave you with Geoff and Ford, Mason. Y'all holler if you need me." Stoney stood, and so did Angie, both of them taking their cups as they went.

"How many cups a week do you guys lose?" Mason asked.

Ford chuckled. "About a dozen. Geoff orders them in bulk."

"Stoney's son builds these crazy structures from the pieces," Geoff added. "He's amazing."

"He is." That deeply happy expression suited Ford to the ground. "How experienced are these guys as riders?"

"I've been assured that they're thrill seekers and both experienced riders."

"Okay. It's a difference of horses that look sleek and expensive versus some slower, more settled mounts."

"Let's go with sleek and expensive. We have a backup plan if the weather's crappy?"

"Geoff has a plan for the food to be under cover, at any rate. Flies. As far as the ceremony, we have huge tents to set up to keep the sun off these folks. We're nearly eight thousand feet closer to the sun than they are. Barring gale force winds or a freak hailstorm, they'll keep the weather off too."

Geoff nodded. "And if that happens, we'll move everyone into the main gathering space. It'll be crowded but doable."

"Sounds great. You guys are tops. The flowers are going to be delicate and frickin' impossible, so they won't be here until the day before or morning of."

"That's fine. Do you have a backup there?"

"Homicide."

"Right. Well, we can always send Tanner off to pick wildflowers and put them in mason jars," Geoff said. "Anyone want brunchy food? I need to cook."

"Sounds good," Ford said, then turned his attention back to Mason. "So, you'll be here from the weekend before the event?"

"If you don't mind. It's not a bad drive, but I'll be putting in some late hours. Someone from the family will arrive Monday or Tuesday, the grooms on Thursday, the rest of the family will be coming Thursday and Friday. The rehearsal dinner is Friday, and we should be out of your hair full-time by Monday."

Mason was already exhausted thinking about it. He took a deep breath, in through his nose, out through his mouth. His phone beeped, the text showing Stoney's number.

You staying the night?

?? Why would Stoney ask that?

Are. You. Staying. The. Night. Asshole.

I can, sure, but I don't want to put you guys out. What the hell?

Massage appt at 8:30 pm. You can use the guest room at the house.

IOU

For a crusty old cowboy, Stoney could be a good man.

"Are you texting with my man?" Ford asked easily. Ranch folks were like small-town folks. They thought nothing of being in each other's business.

"I totally am. He asked me to spend the night, even."

"You're moving fast. I'll make up the guest room. That will give us some real time to look at tent placement."

"And we need to discuss rehearsal dinner menus too," Geoff added. "Mexican?"

He shook his head. "Nothing that will make either guy bloated or acidy, Geoff."

"Ouch. Right. No broccoli or cauliflower, then, either."

"Or asparagus."

"Right. No one wants nasty honeymoon blows."

"Ew!" Ford tossed a piece of walnut at him from the banana bread.

Geoff just pulled out eggs and cheese, sausage and flour. "True, though. I mean, the wedding day menu is tough on the tummy, but you know that's for everyone else. The grooms will barely nibble."

"True. That's really for the pictures." Most couples didn't remember eating their cake at all.

"Not at our wedding," Ford said.

"Yes, well, you boys had two feet of new snow and a very sick mare. Everyone ate as if they were starving." Geoff winked. "It was the most cowboy wedding ever."

"I can only imagine."

"We just had to have it at Christmas," Ford said. "I'm gonna go make up the guest room, okay? You and Geoff make lists."

"We're on it. Thank you, Ford. I appreciate it. The massage will make the difference between me being a sane man and me going postal."

"Well, none of that." Ford clapped him on the back when he went by, leaving Mason with Geoff.

"Are you okay?" he asked Geoff, who was putting together a quiche.

"I'm good. Excited about such a big party, but good."

"So what's with the nervous cooking?"

Geoff paused, then turned a rueful smile on him. "Naked yoga men. I am dying here."

"Ah. I do understand. The well is… a little dry."

"Right? And these guys are all stunning. They're also guests." Geoff sighed dramatically.

"Ah, is that a rule?"

"No one's ever said, 'Geoff, no touchy,' but it's sort of unwritten, you know? Like, would you boff a client's dad?"

"No. That makes for a bad reputation."

"Right? Now, the masseuse guys? They're colleagues. But they're so darned busy they don't have the time."

"I have an appointment for eight thirty."

Geoff grinned over. "Are you going to be naughty, Mason?"

"I certainly hope so." Truth was, he was too tired, but he might have a nap midday. He could, and no one here would tell on him.

"Good for you." Geoff popped the quiche in the oven. "So, we'll need some fun meals leading up to the wedding itself, right?"

"We will. A lot of the core family guests will be here two or three days in advance. Apparently the father of the… well, the Wright daddy. He stayed here when it was a hunting lodge with Ty. He'd like some game meat. One of the grooms was very excited that you could make the Colorado-style pizza."

"I totally can. Ford would love that. I'll put it on the menu. They do understand we don't have a serve-to-order kitchen, right?"

"They do. I explained all meals will be family style. I've tapped the Roaring Fork Bakery to help with making sure we always have snacks. I imagine you'll need sandwiches and nibbles through the day, just like you do now, only on a larger scale."

"Ford says he's hiring me a staff of waiters and a couple of sous chefs."

"Good deal. I might see if one of the bakers can come up and hang out. You do great stuff, but anything we can do to ease your load…." He smiled at Geoff, who was a damned good friend.

Geoff came to him, held his hand a second. "This is a big deal, huh?"

"Huge. I've never done anything this big, and I can't mess it up. I just can't." He'd sunk weeks into this, turned down other jobs.

"I'll make sure it's good, honey. I swear. Ford and Stoney are working their asses off too."

"I can tell. We'll make it happen." Maybe they'd even get into some magazines. The family was bringing in a photographer from… somewhere over by Austin. He was famous.

He started making lists—get tux cleaned, make sure the cake was on point, get the Mr. and Mr. pillows from the… embroiderer? Embroidery lady? From Hazel.

Geoff added all sorts of stuff, and Angie came back up to talk horses and trail rides and so on.

By the time the quiche was ready, he was hungry and the kitchen was full of people and laughter again. There was a real rhythm to life on the ranch, which was great for guests and working folks alike.

And if there were a few naked yoga guys to ogle, well, that was okay too.

Chapter Three

THE drive from Denver to Glenwood Springs was one of the most beautiful vistas Noah Wright had ever seen. That was a good thing, because it soothed the growly mood having to fly to Colorado a week early had caused him.

Seriously, his schedule was slam-packed, but Daddy had suffered a minor heart attack last month, and instead of flying, he was going to ride with Uncle Tom and Aunt Cindy.

Noah rolled his head on his neck and hunted for the turnoff on the state road that led to the Leanin' N. Apparently one could get there from Glenwood-ish or from the Aspen area.

God, it was pretty up here. Cold for June but damn pretty, and the sunshine was something special. The road wound up out of the canyon, gaining elevation, the red rock giving way to more alpine stuff.

At least Sammy had decided to get married somewhere in the States. He would have had a hell of a time organizing this in Mexico.

He checked the GPS, which had gone suspiciously quiet. Twenty miles. Okay. Man, no wonder the planner had said they'd shuttle folks in from Aspen.

Daddy had been talking about this place for ten years, at least, just on and on about how pretty it was, how the hunting was good. Noah wasn't much of a hunter, but he did love to photograph wildlife when he got some rare time away, so he'd take it.

He turned off on a county road, then finally a ranch road with a cattle guard at the gate. A tiny thrill went through him, because this was perfect for Sammy's wedding. Just amazing.

He hit the button at the electronic gate, and he heard, "Leanin' N Ranch, this is Miranda. How can I help you?"

"Hey. I'm Noah Wright, with the Wright/Preston party."

"Mr. Wright. Of course. I'll buzz you in. You can park at the main house, and someone will be out to meet you."

"Thank you." He hoped the main house was clearly marked…. Noah had seen his share of ranches, but this took his breath away.

The gate slid open, not a rattle to be heard, and he headed in. The place was a little compound, with cabins dotting the area and a vast main house that was absolutely welcoming—there was a huge porch with rockers, and fire pits and chimineas placed here and there.

He'd bet they got cold as a witch's tit up here in the winter, but right now it looked like heaven, which was a good start. Maydell had been worried after dealing with the assistant or office manager or whatever he was with Rustic Romance. Apparently the guy was a little flittery and intense. Kinda citified too, which always made his Maydell deeply suspicious.

She'd moved to Dallas from Royse City thirty-plus years ago and still considered herself a small-town girl.

He took a couple of pictures and sent them to her and Sammy both, just so they could see.

He parked at the house, sitting behind the wheel a few moments to stare. A little blond hard body and a skinny cowboy were heading across the porch, obviously chatting. Noah admired the view, hoping they didn't notice him right away. This was better than dinner and a movie.

The cowboy laughed at something Mr. Short and Studly said, and damn, that was a picture and a half.

They both turned just then to look at him, and he was caught by bright blue eyes, rivaling the Colorado sky above them. Lord. Pretty.

Okay, man. Get your ass out of the car.

He popped the door open, and damned if Blond and Beautiful didn't trot out to meet him. "Mr. Wright?"

"That's me."

"I'm Mason O'Reilly. I've been coordinating the wedding."

"Pleased to meet you." He shook hands with Mason, then went for a wry grin. "Can you show me to a restroom?"

"I can. Please, come with me." They headed into the house and off to the right. There was a huge open room with windows that let light pour in, the whole place covered in shelves of books and sturdy furniture, a giant fireplace along one wall. "Right down that hall, first right. If you hit the dining room, you've gone too far."

"Thanks." He liked the look of the ranch so far. Rustic but comfortable, and more modern than he'd been led to believe. He found the bathroom, which held sleek fixtures and Western art behind glass.

Okay, this was nice. He'd seen the random picture, but they hadn't done the place justice. He should have looked them up, sure, but he was busy, and really, this was what Sammy had wanted.

He washed up, then made his way back out and found Mason waiting for him in the great room. "Would you like to put your bags in your cabin?" Mason asked, looking bright-eyed as a chipmunk.

"I guess so. Y'all do a lot of events here?"

"We do. They're family, and this is a glorious space."

"It's nice. This isn't where the reception will be, though, right? It's way too small." He didn't want to come off critical, but the space was tiny for two hundred or more.

"No. No. There's an outdoor venue with tents and fly covers that we're going to use."

"Okay." He glanced out one of the big windows. "If it rains?"

"The tents are strong and sturdy. Unless there's a hurricane, we're covered."

"Right. I just need to check plan B and plan C. Sammy will freak right out if weather ruins her day."

"O-of course." O'Reilly stumbled over the edge of a rug.

"You okay?" He reached out to steady the guy.

"Yes. Clumsy. Let me introduce you to one of the owners, Stoney River."

The cowboy from earlier stood in a doorway that clearly led to a dining and kitchen area. "Hey, there. Stoney River. Pleased. How was your drive?"

"Good. Good. It was farther than I thought from the airport."

"Well, Grand Junction is closer, and they do have direct service from Dallas, but rental cars are much more scarce, and it's a pretty drive in the summer." Stoney chuckled. "You ever come up in the winter, come into the Junction."

"You sound like you might know a little bit about Dallas, hmm?"

"Just a bit. I came up to New Mexico to go to college and never went back down." Stoney chuckled. "Coffee?"

"Lord yes, please." They wandered out of the great room and through a huge dining room and into a warm, comforting kitchen that was set up with a huge farm-style table, where a young man sat and studiously wrote on a tablet.

"This is my son, Quartz. Quartz, this is Mr. Wright."

"Hello, Mr. Wright. It is very nice to meet you." The boy wouldn't quite meet his eyes and didn't offer his hand, but Noah got the sense that it wasn't a bit of rudeness.

No, he thought maybe Quartz was a little… what did Sammy call it? She had an early education degree. On the spectrum?

"How do you take your coffee?" O'Reilly asked.

"Black, please. Thank you."

"No problem." The guy looked stressed as hell, but hey, wedding for over two hundred, right?

He didn't even want to be here, much less organize it. He had work to do. He had his laptop in the car. As soon as he saw the menu and the rest of the venue, he was holing up in his room and staying there.

"So, we have two cabins that are connected, and we thought we'd give those to the grooms and then have the others for the wedding party and the family," Stoney said.

"The grooms?" Noah blinked. "You mean the bride and groom, right?"

The cowboy blinked right back. "Of course. Sorry. I was tongue-tied there for a second. Quartz, can you go find Geoff and Uncle Ford for me?"

"Okay." Quartz stood up and gave him a half smile before leaving the room.

O'Reilly stood with his back to them, making coffee.

"Is everything okay?" How long did it take to make coffee? His senses—which had gotten him through a shitload of business deals and one particularly hinky merger—were telling him something was off.

"Fine. Sorry. Just dealing with details. Lots of details." O'Reilly handed him a coffee cup with the Leanin' N logo over top a rainbow.

He stared at the cup for a moment, alarm bells ringing. "Hmm."

"Let me show you to your cabin, Mr. Wright, and I'll let you get settled." O'Reilly gave him a look that was pure fake calm.

Noah raised one brow, a habit that drove his sister nuts. "I would rather you tell me what's going on."

"A wedding, I hope. There's been a bunch of planning for it not to be." O'Reilly smiled brightly. "Come on, let me show you your cabin. I think you'll love it. Then I can give you a tour."

Oh, something was so going on here. Noah rose, taking his coffee with him. He had a feeling getting this one alone would make him much more forthcoming. "Lead the way."

"Of course. Stoney? Key?"

"On it. You're in a premium cabin. It's the best cabin save the bride and groom ones. If y'all want to meet me out there, I'll meet you."

"Absolutely. It's a lovely accommodation. I think you'll be incredibly comfortable." O'Reilly had this tiny bit of hysteria going on.

Stoney didn't come with them, and Noah waited until they were well outside before grabbing O'Reilly's arm. "Tell me."

"Pardon me?"

He hated being lied to. Touching was probably off-limits, but he needed to know what was going on.

"Tell me what's going on, buddy."

"Look, Mister. Back off. No manhandling the staff." *Ooh. Touchy.*

He held up both hands. "Fine. Sorry. I'm a little stressed because you think my sister is a dude."

"Everything is going to be perfect for your sister's wedding. Trust me."

"I want to do that, Mr. O'Reilly, but I'm getting a bad feeling that someone screwed up. Samantha Wright is my sister. She has six bridesmaids. This may be rainbow central, but she's not a second groom."

"Perhaps if anyone at any point had contacted us using her full name, it might have saved some confusion."

"Did you ask?" He could chew on Maydell later, because she sure deserved it, but damn. "Didn't you have to get her full name for invitations and the guestbook and all?"

"I didn't handle the invitations, your people did, and no. This is a gay resort. I was told Sammy. I had no reason to question."

Noah stared at the guy, who stared back at him. No way was he taking any of the blame for this debacle. No way.

"This used to be a hunting lodge. My daddy talks about it all the time. I had no reason to think it was a gay resort."

He could hear the little shit's eyes roll like dice. Noah was going to pick up those eyes and roll them right back.

"Regardless," Noah went on, "you have less than a week before the wedding, and I imagine your theme for the wedding is a little skewed." He was holding back, trying not to be the stereotypical Texan….

"We're fine. Honestly. No worries."

"I'm not sure you get to say that." Noah was starting to get a little bitchy and he knew it, but damn. "No offense, but when you work in customer service, it's wise to acknowledge your client's concerns."

"You have nothing to worry about. Believe me. Your sister is in good hands."

"I would like to hear your plan. Is an hour long enough?"

"For what?"

He took a deep breath, then gave up and put his Texas right out in the forefront. "For me to sit in here and read my assistant the riot act while you get your shit together and outline how you intend to fix this shitshow you call a wedding planner business. I want a full tour and report in one hour, complete with all of the changes you need to make."

"Do you now?" Mr. Short, Broad, and Blond's eyes narrowed. "Well, I tell you what, Mr. Wright. I'll give you an hour to chew whatever you feel the need to. I'll continue to do my job, which is to make sure your sister's day is perfect. If I were you, I'd take a part of that hour to consider what the fuck you think you'll do if I decide to walk off the job because you manhandled me. I guarantee you, even your money would find it hard to put a wedding together from scratch in five days."

Noah's mouth dropped open, and he pushed right into the little butthead's space. "Are you threatening me? Look, I have no doubt Maydell is partly to blame for this, and I admitted it. That doesn't mean you didn't screw up dotting your i's and crossing your t's."

The cowboy appeared like a jack-in-the-box. "I have your cabin ready, sir. Cabin B. It's gorgeous. I think I may have met your daddy too. You look like him, huh?"

"I do." He scowled. "I'll go unpack and all. You'll have something for me in an hour?" He raised that one eyebrow again.

"I'm sure he will. Mason is a miracle worker, I swear to God. Come on with me, sir. I haven't been to Dallas in a dog's age. Has it changed a lot?" Stoney got him moving, and he had to admit, the easy voice didn't sound in the least bit strained or worried, and that soothed him some.

"It's gotten far busier, I imagine." He was already thinking ahead about calling Maydell and maybe even Sammy. Hadn't she raved about this place's website?

"Lord, hasn't everywhere? I went down to Denver the other day with my husband, and I swear to God, it felt like they were living twenty times faster than I am." Stoney handed over what looked like an old-fashioned key. "So, this is the key. It'll get you into the main house area, your cabin, and the main wedding area. There's a website on the tag—just follow the directions, and you can turn the AC on with your phone before you get in, the lights, order food from the kitchen, what have you." Stoney dangled the key in front of the keypad, and the door unlocked. "It'll work if you keep it in your pants too."

He hooted, surprised into the sound. "I try to keep it in my pants whenever possible."

"Good plan. I don't have that problem. Mine's taken." Stoney laughed, the sound wild, tickled as hell.

"So I hear." He liked Stoney, damn it. Noah grinned. "I got some calls to make and such. In about an hour, Mr. O'Reilly is meant to give me a tour."

"Good deal. You come up to the kitchen when you're ready. Geoff is making ice cream, and he wants opinions. I'll have Mason meet you there." Stoney held out one hand. "Don't you worry. This wedding is fixin' to be epic. I swear it."

"Thanks." That was, at least, not blowing smoke up his ass. He shook hands, then tried the key thing on his cabin.

Worked like a charm. He sure hoped that was a sign.

If it wasn't, he was going to tear O'Reilly a new asshole.

With his teeth.

Chapter Four

"WHAT the fuck happened, man?" He was going to kill Trev. Dead. "How did we not know this?"

"I swear to you, boss. That woman never—never once—said Samantha. She even talked about the rainbows on the website, boss. Of course she knew!"

"I want you to comb every email and contract we did with these people. Make sure there's nothing, *nothing*, they can get us on. That's in your copious spare time. In your work time, I need a bridal bouquet in yellow roses and a central sunflower, along with some bluebonnets if you can get them."

"But—"

"Now." He hung up the phone and called the Roaring Fork Bakery. "Caroline, we have an emergency."

It took five minutes to switch the two grooms topper, to add a metric fuckton of sunflowers and lace to the cake, and to make it a single, less gay-porny groom's cake.

He needed to make a checklist. He turned in a circle, trying to remember where his laptop was. Ford came running in. "Cabins! Tell me what to do for the bride."

"Get rid of the Mr. and Mr. pillows. We need to make sure the toiletries are appropriate. Check the cornhole games." He closed his eyes and breathed. "How the fuck did this happen?" How had he gotten into this? Why the hell did he let the Texan get under his skin?

Mason was a professional. He'd had way worse. Way. There was that time he'd had a wedding planned at the Strater in Durango and the elevator went out. Or the family reunion of sweet, very elderly born-again Christians he'd had planned for six months when the hotel event manager rented the rest of the building to a BDSM convention....

It was that hand on his arm, like he could be manhandled, like this was his fault and he could be pushed into panic. *Fucker.*

He took one deep breath, then another. Ford was still there. "I can work on the bridesmaids' and groomsmen's stuff. You get the bridal cabin. I need about a hundred yards of rose yellow tulle. Can someone call that fabric shop in Glenwood?"

"On it. Can your assistant drive out there?"

"If he can't, he won't be my assistant by 5:00 p.m. He is currently on the top of my shit list."

"I'm sorry, man." Ford squeezed his shoulder. "I got my phone. Call me if you need me before I come back up."

"I'm going to let Stoney deal with Wright. He's good at it."

"Good deal." Ford's laughter trailed back at him. "I always let Stoney deal with the Texans."

"Right on."

"Oh, I don't think so. This is your fuckup. You deal with me. I like Stoney." Tall, Dark, and Asshole stood there in the doorway like he was made to be there. "I want a sitrep. Now."

Mason took a step back, putting space between him and Noah Wright. "I am a professional, Mr. Wright, and I will be treated as such. I apologize for the error, but I am in the process of dealing with every detail." He fought the urge to cross his arms.

"Well, then, you can explain to me what you're doing. Easy peasy."

"Right now I'm going to make a phone call to a fabric store in Glenwood, if you'll excuse me for two minutes." The bastard had given him an hour, for fuck's sake. He had seven minutes left.

"Sure. I'll take a cup of something. The kitchen is that way?"

"It is. Geoff is making ice cream." He tapped his headphone and called the fabric shop, made that order, then called Trev to get him moving. "They're going to have tulle, lace, and a bunch of silk flowers. Grab it and get it here, ASAP."

"I will. I'll be there in a few hours." Trev sounded reasonably cowed.

"Make it an hour and a half, tops."

"Boss."

"Now!" he snapped. Where the hell was his tablet?

Stoney came in, reaching out to squeeze his arm gently. "Breathe, man. Breathe."

"What the hell happened here, Stoney?" This was supposed to be his big break. He hadn't fucked up a little bit. This was huge.

"How bad is it, man? Seriously. We're fixing the cornhole boards, the cake and flowers are on line, the cabins just need a little girl-i-fying and adjusting. What do you think? The big cabin with the little conference room cleaned out for the bride and her girls, put them in the cabins clustered around her, and then put the guys in the rustic chic things in the back?"

"Can you get a couple of couches moved into that conference room?" If they pushed the tables back along the walls and draped the shit out of everything….

"I can move heaven and earth in four days. We got this. This feller just set you off. He needs to bluster, and you need to have an answer for every question instead of just saying you're on it. That's all."

"Right. Right. We've got this. No problem."

Stoney nodded and grinned at him, all crookedy.

Mason had to laugh, but he kept it low. And now he had thirty seconds. Fifteen. Ten. He walked to the kitchen, evincing calm.

"…butter pecan, and then there's a cherry nut. Are any of the guests vegan? I can make a coconut milk based dark chocolate that's orgasmic."

Geoff was his hero.

"No one is vegan, but we do have one vegetarian who doesn't eat eggs. Milk, yeah, but not eggs."

"Let's do the dark chocolate, then. That will be safe all around."

"Sounds good. I have to tell you, this is an amazing cookie."

Looked like food soothed the savage businessman.

"I'm glad you like them. I have them here all the time. I've never met a hater."

"No? I bet my Aunt Ginnie will automatically hate them, then. She's a tough nut."

"We'll find something she likes, then, won't we, Geoff?" He stepped into the room with a smile. "Is there any of the pecan? The smell is stunning. I just want a bite."

"Here you go." Geoff served him up a tasting portion.

"Thank you." He offered Geoff a smile, then asked Mr. Fuckhead, "Which is your favorite so far?"

"Cherry nut." Wright didn't smile back, but he looked more relaxed.

"Exceptional. Did you want to continue your taste test or start your tour?" See him. See him be the calmest ever.

"I'll taste. This is too good to give up." Now Wright did smile, and God, the expression lit up his whole face.

Too bad Mason knew now that the guy would probably kick his ass as well as deal with it. He was pretty but kinda deadly like a moth or a caterpillar or something....

The idea made Mason grin back.

Look at them, smiling like idiots.

"See? Ice cream, the great lactose-driven equalizer." Geoff chuckled softly. "Does your sister like strawberry? Strawberry champagne sorbet sounds perfectly wedding-y."

"It does. And she loves Poteet strawberries."

What the hell was that? Poteet? Shit. Mason did not need another impossible mission.

"Oh, that's grand!" Geoff beamed at Wright like he wasn't the world's biggest turd. "I'll make some up as a surprise."

"You're a miracle worker, buddy," he muttered under his breath before shutting himself up with a bite of ice cream.

Wright's eyes narrowed, but he didn't call Mason on anything. He just ate a cherry out of the bowl Geoff had on the counter.

"Did you find your cabin to your liking?" he asked.

"It's great," Noah conceded. "Really great, and the bed is amazing."

"This is a fabulous resort." Ah, small talk. He didn't have time for this. "I've got a few things to deal with. Holler at me when you want your tour."

"I can go now if I can take this with me." Noah held up another taster cup of ice cream.

"I trust you, Mr. Noah. You can take it."

Dammit, Geoff.

"Lead on, then." Wright gestured for him to go ahead.

His phone beeped, and Mason pulled it out to check.

Bride cabin ready enough to inspect.

U rock, he shot back.

"Would you like to start with the bridal cabin, Mr. Wright? There are still a few odds and ends to complete, of course."

"Of course." The tone was heavy with irony. "Why not?"

"We've got your sister in this larger cabin. There's a sitting area attached where she can have her bridesmaids in privacy and comfort."

"That sounds nice. What were you going to do with it with two grooms?"

"A bathhouse, of course." *Goddamn it, Mason! Stop that shit.* "Seriously, it was going to be a sitting area for the wedding party."

"Just more… manly?"

Was that teasing? He thought maybe that was teasing, not ugliness.

"Less feminine." He could give as good as he got, for sure.

"My sister does have a pair of brass balls." Wright shook his head. "I have to admit, you're nicer when you loosen up."

"I wouldn't let my clients' big day be ruined. Not under any circumstance." He loved his job, as insane as it was, and he intended to keep his baby business afloat.

"No. No, I bet you wouldn't."

They stepped into the bridal cabin, and Mason sagged a little with relief. The place looked amazing. Redneck, but classy, and understatedly feminine. The bedspreads were a bright white, the bed runner a crisp red gingham.

"Y'all have recovered pretty damn well, considering."

"It's a lovely venue."

"Yeah, but I didn't expect these kinds of results so fast. Okay, show me the sitting area."

"We're still very much in process with that one." He hoped Stoney and Ford had done anything. Anything at all.

"It was really set up for all dudes, then." Wright chuckled. "I'd still like to see the space."

"Of course, Mr. Wright. This way." He opened the door, and the place looked empty—all the tables pushed to the walls and covered with white cloths.

Tanner stood in the middle of the room, a clipboard in his hand, his bowed legs bent like parentheses. "Oh, hey, Mr. Mason. I was just making notes. Is this Mr. Wright? Maybe you can help me, sir. We got a ton of furniture we can move in here. Would your sister like lodgepole pine better, or would she like dark wood antique stuff?"

"Lodgepole pine. Absolutely."

Wright's confident words eased him just a little more. That meant even more of his plans would work. This was a redneck.... The saddles. They needed to make sure the tack was white and black, not black and black.

He tugged out his phone and made a note. "The Pendleton blanket cushions, Tanner. Lots of places to sit, the one mini fridge for the wine bottles."

"Yes, sir."

He added wineglasses to the beer glasses he'd already planned on, plus something suitably charming for a wedding morning breakfast. Maybe Texas toast french toast or even something more Colorado. He'd talk to Geoff. "Is there anything she would like for snacks? A music selection for the room? We have all sorts of wireless capabilities, so we could just put in an Amazon Echo...."

Wright rolled his eyes. "Just handle it. She's in Tibet right now. She doesn't even land in the country until Wednesday."

"Of course." It was like coordinating ghosts with money.

"Okay. When they filled out the paperwork, they did indicate a fondness for Miranda Lambert. Oh! Speaking of paperwork, I understand there's to be a canine ring bearer. Is he all right with horses?"

"I have... a what?"

"A canine. A dog?" He spread his hands. "They indicated a hound of some sort, so I think we'll need a leash if that's the case."

"Oh, for fuck's sake. Seriously? Sammy has a ten-year-old basset. You'll be lucky if Frankenfurter doesn't eat the cake, fart, and fall asleep in the aisle walking down it."

"Does he need a top hat with a sunflower on it?" A basset hound. Named Frankenfurter. Sounded fun. And totally out of his control.

"Only if you duct tape it to his head. They take a Christmas card picture of him every year. He wears the headband long enough for them to snap a pic, then flings it off and demands his treat."

"I'm on it." So, headband, dog treats, poop bags, dog wrangler. He'd pay Stoney's son twenty dollars an hour for the privilege. "Did you want to see the groom's quarters and the yurts?"

"Yurts. You bet I do." Wright was looking downright tickled now, which worried Mason more than a little.

The Tickled Texan. That could be a book. Maybe it already was.

It was probably porn.

"Come with me. Tanner, thank you. I'll be back in ten to match our lists."

"You got it." Tanner tipped his hat. "Pleasure to meet you, sir."

"Same." Wright followed Mason out into the sunshine just as Ford popped out of the old bunkhouse where the bridesmaids would be staying.

"Well, hey! I'm Ford Nixel. You must be Noah Wright. Pleasure to meet you. We're in the process of luxe-ing it up in here for the ladies if you want to come see."

Ford looked... stunning. The man was covered in glitter and strings, and Mason was fairly sure there were flower petals in his hair. He had to snap a picture of this. Had to.

Stoney would never forgive him if he missed it.

He took the photo just as Ford and Noah Wright shook hands. Nice.

Ford glared for half a second over Wright's shoulder, and Mason smiled.

Yeah, yeah. He had to do it.

Wright followed Ford into the long low building, leaving Mason to breathe a moment. He texted Trev. *Where are you?*

Glenwood. Do you want this too? A picture popped up of embroidered denim covered in wildflowers.

God yes. They could totally work with that. If nothing else, they could cover some pillows in it.

Good deal. Be there soon.

He nodded and jogged over to the cabin where Tanner was working. They needed to deal with the tack and make sure there were carpets down where the bride was mounting.

The bride. Christ. He hadn't done a straight wedding in two years.

"Hey." Tanner's face lit up with a smile when Mason ducked inside. "What a thing, huh?"

"You have no idea, man. Talk about a rude shock, huh?"

"Yeah. Good thing we have all that girly stuff from those two ladies who got married in April."

"I'm not sure Miss Val would appreciate being called girly…." Stoney walked in with an armful of vases. "She made Angie look like a fairy."

"They still had dainty stuff compared to what we were doing for this one." Tanner checked something off his list. "What you need, Mason?"

"Tack. Do we have something more feminine than not?"

"If we don't, Angie will know where to find something on the fly. We have a couple of days for that." Stoney winked at him. "Mason's hiding from the big, bad Texan."

"Shut up." He was not. He was working. "He's with your man. See?" Mason queued up the picture on his phone.

Stoney's lips twisted; then the grin got bigger. "Oh, that's precious. Quartz is going to ride his ass for days."

"Right?" He might have to print this out and give it to Stoney to hang in the breakroom at the ranch house.

"So, are you feeling a little less panicked, buddy?"

"Fortunately a wedding is a wedding, and this one is a redneck… the mason jars. Fuck." He grabbed his phone. "Trev! Stop at the Target and buy me a box of mason jars—if they have the ones with handles, buy two. Then get me an assortment of shit to make bride and groom cups. Etching, chalkboard tape, glass paint. Whatever you can find. Grab a cake server from the bridal department too."

"I'll get one of everything." Trev sounded out of breath but cheerful. Trev did love to shop.

"I have plenty of ribbons of all sorts in that tote in the car, so we're good there." The birdseed bundles were all done already, the enamelware would work no matter what, and everything was labeled Sammy and Doug that he could think of.

He'd double-check that when Trev arrived.

"Okay. I got the tulle at the fabric shop, so I won't get any cut stuff here. I'm going to buy some gift bags just in case." He could hear Trev's panic easing, and that made Mason want to whap the little shit.

"Grab me two twelve-packs of Diet Dr Pepper and a Snickers bar?"

Geoff would fuss, but he needed the boost.

Chapter Five

THE clusterfuck that had been going on when he arrived was well taken care of, and Noah would never admit it to hot little Mason O'Reilly, but by the day Sammy and Doug were supposed to show, he was suitably impressed.

Maydell arrived first, pulling up in a jaunty little Jeep she'd rented at Enterprise. Sammy and Doug were driving up with Frank the hound. Their ring bearer. Holy shit.

Maydell looked suitably cowed, he thought, even though she maintained she hadn't done a thing wrong. Noah had jogged out to the parking lot to meet her, carry her bags inside.

Now she was sitting in the front room of the ranch after her long nap, her feet on a stool, a fire in the fireplace. In June. "When did you say Momma and Daddy were coming in?"

"They're leaving Denver first thing in the morning, and your Uncle Tom is flying in to drive them in. I imagine fully half of the flights coming into Grand Junction are for this."

"I bet." He chuckled, thinking how those airport folks would think there was an invasion of north Texans and a metric shit-ton of UT alumni.

"Is there anything you need me to do? Did you tell me this place was going to shuttle us back and forth to Aspen?"

"The Friday night of the rehearsal dinner and Saturday all day."

"Well, that will be a real help."

Noah nodded. "They'll also have vans up from the parking area down at the main road."

Stoney came walking in, carrying a tray of drinks and nibbles. "At least it's not snowing. We'd have to use the sleigh."

"It's *June*!" Maydell sounded like Stoney had just whipped his dick out in front of her.

"Yes, ma'am. We don't feel safe until after the Fourth of July."

"And then only until Labor Day." Ford Nixel walked in, dapper as always. "Good afternoon, ma'am. Welcome to the Leanin' N." He reached out and kissed her hand when she offered it over.

She fluttered a little, her smile wide. "Pleased to meet you. Now, what do you boys need me to do?"

Stoney presented the tray. "Try these canapés?"

"Oh, y'all." She took one, then began to fan herself. "Lovely. Is that barbecue?"

"It is. Geoff got a smoker for Christmas. That's our chef. You can meet him on the tour."

Noah let the guys entertain Maydell and moved off to touch base with Sammy. He texted her: *Where y'at?*

Aspen. Having coffee and a puppy pee break.

Good deal. Ready to get this show on the road.

Is it beautiful?

Stunning. Maybe not like Tibet.

Tibet was kinda sad in places, Ark. So filled with rich people's trash. This will be better.

He didn't remind her that it was the Wright fortune that allowed her to wander around the world being philanthropic. Nor did he point out that the cost of this wedding could probably feed a small third-world country. He would, but Momma and Daddy were on their way and might just kill him.

Besides, he had plenty of time after she got married to poke and prod her into running the charity arm of Wright International. Then she could do good in a tangible way and have babies at the same time. At least that's what she wanted the last time they spoke. You never knew with Sammy.

I'm here waiting for you. Hurry up.

Frank is old, Ark. Be there in an hour.

Right. He looked around for O'Reilly. "Where the hell is he?"

"Who?" Stoney looked honestly confused.

"Wedding planner. Shouldn't he be here?"

"His name is Mason," Ford said drily. "He's in the kitchen with Geoff. They're playing alchemy or something."

"Be right back. I have to make sure he's dealt with a few things."

"Sure." Stoney gave him that look, the one he knew as Texan for "Be nice."

Apparently Mr. Not-So-Into-Research was stressing it a little.

Too bad. He was paying O'Reilly for a single perfect experience, and he wanted it done right. Noah headed to the kitchen, not even sure why he was ready to tear the guy a new asshole. He just was, all of a sudden.

He turned the corner, and as he expected, O'Reilly was in the kitchen. What he didn't expect was for him to have his head on the table, sleeping away.

Geoff glanced up from where he sat at his little command center making notes, and smiled. He put a finger to his lips. "He just needs a catnap," Geoff whispered.

He felt his eyebrow rise and rise and rise. "Sammy is going to be here in less than an hour! This is her wedding, and the man I'm paying to handle everything is *asleep on the job*?"

Noah slammed his hand down on the table, and Mason stood straight up, stumbling back a few steps before Geoff caught him.

"Wh-what do you need, Mr. Wright?"

"I need you to be on the damned ball. Maydell is here. Sammy is in Aspen. Where do we stand? Have you dealt with someone to watch the dog? She's bringing him, but he's going to need constant supervision."

"Quartz is willing, and Stoney has assigned a hand to help. Would you like to meet him? His name is Avery, and apparently he's had bassets." Mason was standing up straight now and frowning.

"Yes, they'll be here in an hour." He wanted to make sure someone was going to be available.

"Give me a couple of minutes to text him."

"Thanks." Noah refused to feel bad, even if Geoff was staring.

"You, uh, hungry?" Geoff asked.

"No." No, he was surprisingly nervous. This was his baby sister, and he was in charge of all this. If it was messed up, no one would remember anything but that it was his fault. "Are there snacks available for when they get here?"

"You bet. Those ones I sent to Maydell were the experiments. Stoney said she seemed the barbecue type." Geoff's gaze was surprisingly knowing.

"She is. They'll be coming in fits and starts from now on. My parents, my aunts and uncles, my granny. Doug has his folks and three brothers, his grandfather."

"It's going to be so much fun!"

"A joy." God, he didn't know if he could do this.

Mason came over to put a hand on his arm, almost shocking him to death right there. "Have some brisket. I'll go grab Avery and Quartz. I'll double-check the bride and groom cabins and make sure your folks have everything in place. Your uncle will be staying in Aspen?"

"Yeah, he has friends there."

"Well, if he's too tired, we'll still have room for him up until the rehearsal." Mason bustled off.

Geoff whipped him up a plate of brisket crostatas with hot barbecue mustard sauce and a dab of coleslaw on top, as well as miniature corn muffins stuffed with jalapeno relish and the tiniest chicken-fried steak bites he'd ever seen on toothpicks.

"This is amazing."

"Just a sampling of the wedding reception. A teaser, if you will."

"I like it." He better than liked it. If he thought there was a chance in hell, he would try to hire Geoff as a personal chef. Noah thought he knew better. In the last week or so, he'd seen how loyal people were to the Leanin' N.

"Good. Now stop growling at Mason because you're scared. He's doing a kickass job. Also, would you like some iced tea?"

"I would. He was napping."

"Yeah. We do that a lot. Find five minutes to rest in between waves. He was up all night last night and the night before. He's a good guy." Geoff gave him a raised eyebrow, something Noah did often enough to know he was being chastised. "I know you two got off on the wrong foot, but, really, let him do his thing. That's why you hired a wedding planner."

"He's not half-bad at all," he conceded. Hell, the man had managed to add the bride into this wedding pretty easily.

Sammy would never know unless he told her. Noah thought maybe he would do that on her first anniversary. Then again, you never knew what was gonna pop out of his mouth when she made him nuts.

Hell, he was more worried about his daddy showing up here and having a meltdown, especially after all the buildup about the hunting lodge that was.

The Leanin' N was a totally different animal now, he thought.

Mason returned in just minutes bringing young Quartz and a fresh-faced cowboy with a strawberry blond cowlick and a crop of summer freckles that put Poteet strawberries to shame.

"This is Avery. Avery, Mr. Wright."

"Hi." Avery stuck out a hand, callused and beat to hell, belying his age. "I'm going to be your dog wrangler, I hear. Pleased."

The young man hung back, quiet and still, not meeting his eyes much. He liked Quartz just fine, though, and Noah never tried to push.

"I hope you're still pleased when you meet the saggy fartbag."

That made the kid laugh, and Geoff and Avery joined right in. "I like dogs. I take care of them here every day for Daddy and Uncle Ford."

Noah had seen an array of border collies and Aussies. Ranch dogs. He got that. But if the kid took care of fast, motivated dogs like that, he could handle Frank. "Good deal. The big thing is he's not used to going out without a leash. He follows his nose and can get lost."

"We have a nice fenced play area for dogs too," Avery said. "Lots of folks bring their pups up, and not all of them are off-leash types."

Quartz nodded, more enthusiastic now. "We made an agility course for them to play on."

"Oh, wow." He had a moment of pure joy picturing old Frank running agility, ears flapping, tongue lolling. "He's sort of old, you know…."

"It's okay. No one will be mad if he doesn't want to. Everyone has different abilities."

"That's so true." That was a damned good sign in a kid like Quartz. Someone was teaching him right.

"Anyway, you just have someone holler at us when they get here, and we'll whisk… Frank?" When Noah nodded, Avery went on. "To the lap of doggie luxury. No worries at all."

"Thank y'all. Really. She loves that dog to death."

"All dogs deserve that." Avery chuckled. "Geoff, you got anything for a starved cowboy?"

"I have grilled pimento cheese sandwiches for both of you."

"Yay!" Quartz moved to a cabinet and pulled out two chipped old plates.

"What do you mean, for both of them? Are you holding out on me, man? I thought we were friends." Noah loved pimento cheese.

"I can hook you up." Geoff winked. "Quartz, can you pour Mr. Wright a glass of iced tea while I make sammies?"

"Yes, Geoff." An old, heavy glass appeared from another cabinet, this one in easy reach for a lad much younger than Quartz. Quartz poured a glass of tea, then got two more cups to fill with milk from the big fridge.

"Have you lived here your whole life, Quartz?"

"Yes, sir. I was born here."

"Wow. That's pretty cool."

"Uh-huh. This is a good place, isn't it, Geoff?"

"Yes, sir. The best."

Mason chuckled, which only made Noah realize he'd been gone again. "Can I get a sandwich too?"

"Of course. Another cup of coffee?"

"Please."

The plates were filled with sandwiches, and Geoff kept making them as people kept showing up. There must have been a dozen ranch hands and a couple of what looked like waitstaff already in, maybe for room service? He had no idea. Watching all the bustle calmed him down, and soon enough, Ford and Stoney and Maydell were in the big kitchen as well.

"I have to say, Noah, I do like it here," Maydell murmured over her cheese sammie and milk.

"Do you usually allow guests in here?"

"We don't have guests. Only family." Oh, Ford was slick as snot.

Geoff snorted. "I only kick people out when I need to make something that might fall in the oven. Soufflé. Right, Stoney?"

Stoney looked so very innocent.

Oh, there was a story and a half, he'd bet.

Ford rolled his eyes, but Maydell laughed out loud. "Soufflés are so picky."

"Yes, ma'am. Finicky even."

A buzz sounded, and Stoney answered his phone. "Hey, lady. Are they? Excellent. Thanks." He hung up before grinning at Noah. "The bride and groom are here, y'all."

Noah hopped up, ready to go see Sammy for the first time in months. "I got this, y'all. Give me a few, huh?"

"Of course." Mason rose, holding out an arm for Maydell. "Shall we go discuss a few things, lady?"

"You aren't fixin' to holler at me, are you?"

"I wouldn't dream of it. Not in a trillion years. I save that for your boss."

"Oh, good." Maydell took Mason's arm, and Noah grinned. That was dear.

Stoney pointed him out the kitchen door, and he headed outside, boots clicking.

Sammy was getting out of her Escalade, her dark hair pulled up in a ponytail, her face tanned and healthy. "Ark! Ark, I missed you!"

"Hey, baby girl." He held out his arms and met her halfway. She ran to him so he could pick her up and swing her around.

She was still a little thing, and her laughter hadn't changed a bit since she was tiny.

"Hey, Noah." Doug was tall and skinny as a rail and looking happy as anything.

"Hey, man. You have a good drive?"

"I did. It's gorgeous up here, isn't it? I couldn't believe how perfect it was when Sammy showed me the website."

Noah paused, then raised a brow at Sammy. "So you did look at the website?"

"Sure. It's gorgeous. Everything that Daddy said but classy."

"And rainbowy." He just needed to know she understood that part.

"Well, sure. It's gay-friendly. Doug's brother is gay, after all. I want him to feel comfortable. I mean, it's not like it's antiheterosexual, right? They're not going to insist I cut my hair and wear flannel, after all."

"Not that I know of." Doug had a gay brother? And they'd never introduced him? Damn.

"Good. So, tell me, is it as beautiful on the inside?"

"It's amazing. Hi, Frank." The basset had lumbered over on his long leash to sniff at his boots. "Y'all hungry?"

"Yes," Doug said.

"No. Not until after the wedding. Momma will skin me if I can't fit in my dress."

"You have to eat, baby girl. You lost ten pounds in Tibet. Momma will skin you if the dress is too big too." He knew Momma's temper.

"See, love? Listen to your brother. He knows." Doug nodded to him.

He grinned and wrapped an arm around Sammy, steering her toward the house.

"Can Frank come in?" she asked. "I mean as soon as he pees?"

"Of course he can, and I have two basset wranglers for him too."

The basset in question farted audibly and then proceeded to water the grounds.

Doug hooted. "You mean I'm not stuck with him the whole weekend?"

"No, y'all can rest assured he's being adored. The wranglers in question are in the kitchen. Come and see." He led her in, feeling a little like a proud papa as he showed off the already decked-out main room and dining area. "We'll have supper in here tonight and tomorrow."

Then they entered the kitchen, where Maydell stood and squealed, "Miss Sammy! Hello!"

"Maydell! Oh, it's good to see you." They hugged and bussed cheeks. "Look at all the hustle."

"This is her, is it?" O'Reilly walked right up and held one hand out. "Mason. I'm here to make whatever you want to happen, happen."

Sammy took Mason's hand in both of hers. "Oh, thank you. This place is amazing, so we're already halfway there. This is Doug, and that's Frank."

"Doug." Mason shook hands with Doug too, then knelt to let Frank sniff his fingers. "Avery?"

"Quartz and I are on it." Avery offered Sammy a warm smile. "Ma'am, this is Quartz River. He'll be loving on Mr. Frank for you."

"Oh? Well, I appreciate your help very much, Mr. River. Frank needs someone to help him not be frightened."

Quartz couldn't quite look up to meet her eyes, but he nodded. "New places can be scary. He's a handsome feller."

"He is, isn't he? He's dear to me." Sammy knelt down and started talking to Quartz, leaving Doug to lean next to him.

"Glad to be here. I tell you what. I'm hoping to keep her at home a few months after the wedding."

"I think you should get her pregnant immediately." He winked when Doug almost choked.

"So does she." That was from Sammy. "We've been practicing long enough."

"I like the idea of being Uncle Ark."

"Ark?" Mason asked.

"As in Noah and the." Sammy laughed.

"When she was a baby, I had an ark in my room— this huge, handmade beast. She loved it and cried for it. Ark! Ark!"

"I guess I started calling him that too. I had nightmares, and I would scream for Noah."

"You still have the ark?" Mason seemed pretty curious, but maybe he was just being polite.

"In the storage room at Momma and Daddy's. For when this one has said babies."

"I promise to do my best."

"I know, kiddo."

"Who wants a sandwich?" Geoff bustled over, wearing the best apron ever. It had buff, half-naked dudes on it wearing chef hats.

"Oh my God. That's precious!" Sammy squealed. "I'd love one. Half of one."

"Sure thing." Geoff enveloped Sammy, then Doug, in huge hugs. "We've all heard so much about you. Everyone sit. Quartz, take the puppy outside?"

"Yes, sir." Quartz took the leash and grabbed a dog biscuit. "Come on, Frank. We can go to the play yard."

The drooly beast focused on the cookie and was off, wagging hard enough that his butt was shaking. Avery followed, and Noah figured Frank was in good hands.

Doug and Sammy ate standing up, citing the long ride as too much sitting. "Besides, I want to see everything!" Sammy said. "Do you have all the decorations and reception fun set up somewhere? I've checked the weather, and we should be good there."

"We have everything ready to go. The tents are up, but we're leaving a lot of the smaller things in the sheds. The cornhole boards, for instance. The magpies and ravens love beanbags." Mason smiled gently. "Anything you want to see, though, I can show you."

For a man who hadn't slept in three days, O'Reilly was damned coherent, seriously.

"Boss! Have you seen the basset in the dog run? He's gorgeous." Trev walked in with his "Jeep Naked" T-shirt and a pair of cutoffs that were tight enough to read his pulse.

"I have. Trevor, this is Doug and Sammy. The wedding couple." Mason's tone went a wee bit stern.

"Oh! Hey. Sorry, I was painting, and I'm a bit underdressed." Trevor held up painty hands.

Shit, Trevor was a bit underdressed for a Pride parade.

"No problem." Sammy blinked a little, and then Stoney's phone went off.

"Looks like some of the groom's people are arriving, along with the best man."

"Oh, Steve-O!" Doug smacked a kiss on Sammy's mouth. "Eat that fruit Geoff gave you. I'll meet them."

Noah watched, just tickled to death. This might work out. Maybe.

Sammy bounced and hugged him. "I can't believe how neat this place is. Are the cabins gorgeous?"

"They are. Come on. I'll show you and let all these guys get back to work."

"Of course." Sammy took Noah's hand. "Mason, will you come with us?"

Mason's brows went up, but he nodded. "Sure."

Oh, there was trouble coming. He knew his sister and her little games. She had something to spring on them, and he would have warned Mason if he'd had time.

"So, we have the doughnut wall and the signage and the cornhole games, right?"

They headed out toward the cabins, Sammy swinging his hand like a little girl.

"Right," Noah agreed. "Everything looks great."

"Cool. So, Dougie and I were talking, and we'd like a bridal climbing wall and a clothesline to display Polaroids that people take at the wedding. Also, I forgot to bring the wedding party gifts, and I want to surprise Dougie after the wedding with some news, so I need a few things."

Noah thought O'Reilly was going to pass out.

"That's a lot to ask last-minute, honey," Noah said. Not that he wouldn't move heaven and earth to get her what she wanted.

"I know, but it's important, Ark. I need pink and blue balloons to fill up the back of the Escalade and a few stork balloons too."

"That's dangerous to drive…." He stopped. "Wait. What?"

Her cheeks were bright pink.

"You just hedging your bets with both colors?" Mason asked.

"It's too early to know. I'm just in early days. I'm not even telling the 'rents."

"Oh my God." Noah lifted her clean off her feet and spun her.

"I know, right? So you two are the official first people I've told. You'll help me, right?"

"Of course we will." Mason tugged out his phone and began making notes, Noah assumed. "Polaroids and film. Balloons. A climbing wall. The bridal gifts… can someone overnight them? I'll have to run into Grand Junction for the rest."

"Oh, that's smart. Yes. Yes, I should have thought about that."

"No climbing wall," Noah said firmly.

"We need a climbing wall, Ark."

"Not if you're pregnant, we don't." He wasn't gonna budge on this.

"No one knows. I was pregnant climbing. Hell, I got knocked up climbing."

"Yeah, well, if your man isn't smart enough to stop you, that doesn't mean I'm not." He glared, lips pressed together.

"Ark… I'll just tell Mason here to do it. He has to make me happy."

Mason shook his head. "It's not my job to get in the middle of this," he teased.

"Oh, yes. I'm the bride. I'm the boss."

They all had a chuckle, but Noah knew that stubborn set of chin. She meant it.

"I'll have to see what I can do. I'm going to have to run to the Junction…."

"I'll come with you, if that's okay." The offer was out before Noah even thought about it. "That way you don't have to expense all these last-minute add-ons."

And he'd be able to ensure she wasn't on the phone to Mason, demanding to bungee jump into the wedding or enter on a bucking bull. Crazy girl. He did adore her, but there was a little one to consider, and it was his job to protect her until Doug could.

"Sure." Mason's expression showed pure shock. "It might be a late night. I'll start making calls to the major retailers to see if they can set aside Polaroid stuff. I'll see you at the house?"

"How long?"

"Ten."

"Done." That would give Noah time to read her the riot act a bit.

"This is the perfect place, isn't it, Ark?"

"It is." He grinned at her. Who was he kidding about kicking her ass? "Seriously, you could have warned me it was a gay resort."

"Seriously, you need to breathe."

"I am. Daddy is going to freak out." Not about the gay, just how different it was.

"Daddy won't freak out, Mr. Uptight Business Guy."

"I am not uptight!" Maybe he was, but someone had to get shit done. Daddy had turned a huge portion of the business over to Noah when he was twenty-five. He had been there when the oil boom had made them billionaires, and now? It was all his.

The pressure drove him out of bed every morning, but it also threatened to give him ulcers some days. So what? That was the price of success.

Sammy stared at him. "Seriously. You aren't uptight. Ark, if a guy shoved a lump of coal up your ass, you'd shit the Hope Diamond."

"Well, I have you to be unconventional and free for me." That sounded more accusatory than he meant it to, and Noah hugged Sammy tight. "I love you, baby girl, and I'm so happy for you."

"I love you, Ark. I want to be happy for you too, okay?"

"What does that mean?" He laughed it off, waving a hand in the air. "I'm fine."

"Uh-huh. It's going to be the best weekend! Have you seen the cake? Do you know if it's strawberry?"

"I think you're going to like it." He knew Geoff was doing something with strawberries, even if the cake lady wasn't.

To be honest, he hadn't asked about the cake.

There was going to be cake, right?

"I need to go, honey. That cabin there is yours. I'm sure there's a key for you." Probably tied with ribbon and lace.

"I'll ask the cowboy guy to let me in. He's cute as hell."

"You're a sick girl." He kissed her cheek, but he needed to hustle, so he left her, noting the dog run, which he'd missed before. Frank was playing ball with a corgi. Ball. Wow.

Maybe this was a magical place….

He shook his head and snorted. Noah didn't believe in magic, but he could appreciate hard work. God knew they had that in spades around the Leanin' N.

Chapter Six

"NO, Trev, I need that climbing wall. I know you can get one in from Aspen." The drive down to Grand Junction was a pretty one at least, winding through DeBeque Canyon. Noah had offered to drive, which left Mason free to make calls and lists and try not to lose his mind.

"Boss. Seriously? A wedding decorated climbing wall?"

"Be grateful she didn't ask for the Wailing Wall, and do it!" he snapped, then hung up. He had ordered balloons and a fresh can of helium, along with random "father to be" crap. They were going to have to stop at three different stores for enough cameras and films, Walmart for the clothespins, Enstrom's for three hundred little boxes of toffee. Fuck.

"What flavor is the wedding cake?"

"What?" Mason glanced at Noah. "I—whatever they asked for."

"You don't know?"

"Trevor dealt with that."

"You didn't taste it?"

Mason was going to hit him. "Let me check my notes."

"I mean, I would guess all of Trevor's taste is in his mouth…."

"Did you just say that?" Mason called up his Google Sheets. "Layers of butter cake with strawberry jam and fresh strawberries, and layers of devil's food with salted caramel icing."

"Oh, thank God." Noah chuckled. "She just mentioned strawberry today, and I panicked a bit."

"She's very important to you. I can tell." He didn't have birth family anymore, but he had his godbaby, his friends, even Trev.

"She is. She's spoiled as fuck, but she makes up for that by being a good person." Noah's smile spoke volumes.

He smiled back, then bent his head to his lists. He texted Geoff about midnight snacks for tonight, texted Stoney to make sure the bride liked her room—although he typed "bridge" and it took a second to decipher: *London Sammy has neither fallen nor complained.*

He sent back: *Oh good.*

"How are we doing on all the stuff we need?" Noah asked, which made Mason blink.

How weird. We. Like they were in this together.

"There are a bunch of stops, but it's doable, I think. I hope."

"You hope?"

"It's doable." *Shut up.*

"Okay. Well, where am I headed first?"

When he glanced up, they were past Palisade and nearing the first Grand Junction exit.

"Get off here. We'll start at this Walmart."

"You got it." Noah took the circular exit off I-70, and they headed in past Clifton to the Walmart on North Avenue.

He had to wonder when the last time Mr. Noah Wright had dragged his ass to a Walmart was. Hell, he had to wonder why Mr. Wright was on this little trip at all.

"Why did you come with me?" he asked, because he was stupid and couldn't control his mouth.

"Like I said, so I could pay." He got a wry glance. "And to keep Sammy from continuing to bitch about my personal life. Or lack thereof."

"Ah." Like that made sense. That didn't make sense. Noah Wright had money, he was a stud and a half, and the man wasn't the meanest guy Mason had ever met.

Not quite, anyway.

"She's just in love with love right now."

"That's perfect, isn't it? Happy brides are… well… happy." He'd dealt with stressed-out grooms, lots of them, and it always landed on the wedding coordinator.

"True." Noah chuckled. "Love seems like a lot of work."

"Parties are a lot of work. Love just lasts longer."

"I guess." Noah didn't sound so sure, and that made Mason a bit sad.

"Trust me. Your girl is out there, waiting for you."

A loud laugh burst out of Noah. "You think so? She'd have to be pretty permissive."

"Oh." Oh dear. He did not need to know the kinks of his, to-date, biggest client.

"Since I only sleep with men." Noah dropped it like a turd in the punch bowl. Boom.

"Christ, I thought you were going to confess that you liked goat fucking or something." He stopped, blinked, then shook his head. *Seriously? Did you seriously just do that? Are you trying to commit professional hara-kiri? Seriously?*

"Not since high school."

There was a long, long pause, and then they both whooped with laughter, Noah slapping the steering wheel with one hand.

They parked, laughter fading, then bubbling up again, both of them howling. They were gonna get the cops called on them or something. Lord.

"They're going to take us away, Mr. Wright."

"You never know. Thanks, Mr. O'Reilly. I needed that."

"You're more than welcome." Right. *Focus. Wedding bibs and bobs. Cameras. Film. Don't get excited because Mr. Wright is gay. He's not for you. Rich Texans do not choose little nebbishy Colorado boys for fun.*

"Come on, let's go get all that film and shit."

Right. They were on a mission. "I'm on it. Let's do a run on film."

They headed into the Walmart like two warriors going into battle. As one, which was better than being at odds, he guessed.

Either that or Noah had never been in a Walmart and was counting on him....

The idea made him chuckle again, an echo of their laughter.

"Come on, you. Get with the program."

Mason nodded. *Right. Right, focus.* He was so tired that the fluorescents made little shapes in the aisles. Still, they just had to wade through to layaway. Everything should be held there.

Thank God for store managers and a credit card with a hefty limit.

Noah paced him through two Walmarts, a Target, a camera shop that stayed open late for them, and one seriously well-stocked CVS.

"Ta-da!" Mason wiped fake sweat off his brow when they left the drugstore. "Twenty cameras and enough film for every guest to take two to three pictures."

Noah laughed, which he'd been doing all evening, the sound warm and happy. "Go us!"

"We just have to hit the party store, and then we can head back." He could grab the balloons and the helium container, and then that would be it, at least until tomorrow.

"Want to stop and have some food before we go?"

He almost shook his head, but his stomach snarled, answering for him. Mason nodded instead. "Balloons Plus has had someone stay for us. We just need to pop in."

"Point me the right way."

Grand Junction rolled up its skirts at dark, so they gathered all the balloons and helium and then headed downtown for a bite to eat—the Rockslide was down there and had fried jalapenos to die for.

They found a place to park and headed into the crowded, noisy bar and restaurant. There was a hang glider at one end of the big main room and rows of booths all done in dark wood.

"Smells amazing in here," Noah said.

"It does. I stop in here quite a bit when I'm in town." Grand Junction was the closest good-sized city to them, so he came in to shop once a quarter or so.

"I like it." They got settled across from each other, and the server explained all the craft beers the place had on tap. "I'll try the amber," Noah murmured.

"Iced tea for me, please." He was so tired that a beer would knock him on his ass.

"You okay with me having a beer?" Noah peered at him over the menu, dark green eyes serious.

"Of course. I'm not a teetotaler. I just know I don't need one, not right now."

"Cool. One won't affect my driving, just in case you worry."

"No. Of course not. It would affect mine." He chuckled, feeling his cheeks heat. It was true, though. He was too pooped to pop.

"You get to sleep after this is over, right?" When he glanced up, the teasing light in Noah's eyes caught him, grabbing his attention.

"I've got a little event in Aspen midweek next week, and then I have a few days off." He knew how to work hard, after all.

"Good deal. My sister can be a challenge. It's been easy up until now."

Lord have mercy, he didn't want to think about the next few days if it was going to get harder than this. He shook his head mournfully. "This wedding's going to be the death of me."

Noah nodded. "You have no idea. You wait. Momma will be here in the morning."

Yeah, there was nothing like the folks coming in. It was always a promise of drama. Maybe he'd get a nap.

"I look forward to meeting them."

"Forces of nature, my folks. I'll get Stoney to take Daddy fishing."

"Is your mom a fisherman?"

"God, no. She'd rather eat a bug. She'll go with him if he goes to the lake or the Gulf, but she'll read and bask." That horrified face made him cackle.

"Maybe I should arrange for a spa day for them…." That would get them both out of his hair for the day and let him work.

"Oh, that would tickle Momma to death." Noah laughed, clapping his hands. "Daddy might just die. I'll take the calzone, hon. Can I just get it with pepperoni?"

"Of course. What would you like, sir?"

"I'll have a bacon cheeseburger, please."

"Fries?"

"Sure. Can you still do the Texas toothpicks? It's not on the menu."

She winked. "It's on the bar menu. I'll have them right out."

"You are made of win." He leaned back and pondered the pendant lights. Why didn't they ever work this well at home?

"You okay?" Noah asked. The touch to the back of his hand made him jump as if a spider had landed on him.

"I am. This is going to be an amazing event." He couldn't fuck this up. This was huge for him.

"It is. I have to say I'm impressed. By you as well as all the guys—"

"And gals."

"And ladies at the ranch, yeah."

"Stoney and Ford run a top-notch organization. You'll be impressed with the bakery as well. They're exceptional." He started clicking down the mental list. "You hired your own photographer, and your preacher is coming, yes?"

"I texted with them both today. We're on schedule."

"Excellent. The buses are on line for Friday and Saturday. Food is in Geoff's hands." They were staying on top of the emergencies. He knew Ford had literally put out a fire in one of the barns today.

He was considering having a tiny breakdown Sunday afternoon.

"Geoff has good food hands." Noah chuckled. "Too bad he's not my type."

"I can tell you this, Geoff will never leave the Leanin' N. Never."

"No? He does seem loyal." Noah sighed dramatically, which was kind of hilarious.

"Well, I'm sure he…. Shit, I don't know what to say, man." What did you say? Offer to hook them up? Grunt like you understand? What? He was tired and wigged-out and, okay, a little pissed, because goddamn it, why didn't anyone ever get a hard-on for him?

"What is there to say?" Noah winked at him. There was a lot of winking going on.

"Right. Are you going to be able to do something fun tomorrow?"

"Oh, I imagine I'll be there to help do whatever you need. Sammy and Doug will toss out a million dumb ideas."

"That's normal." Dammit.

"But it will be my job to tell them no for you. This was our one big gesture, you see."

Now it made more sense why Noah had come with him. Mason would bet Noah would leverage this with Sammy, pointing out how much time and effort her few additions to the plan had cost them.

"I don't envy you." His job was to say "yes" and "absolutely" and "I'll make it happen."

"You've seen what an ass I can be. I can do it."

Their toothpicks came, a pile of fried goodness with ranch—and *that* they could bond over. *Oh God, so good.*

"Okay, you get a bonus just for this. Tell me we get these at the wedding."

"Yes, sir." *Note to self: Texas toothpicks for the wedding.* Geoff could do anything the Rockslide could do. He wondered what Noah would think of honey cheese bread from Beau Jo's.

Not that there was a Beau Jo's in Glenwood any longer, damn it.

Maybe he'd go to Idaho Springs next weekend. He did love a salad bar in a bathtub. That and the honey cheese bread….

"You with me?" Noah asked. "I mean, I know I'm not the ideal dinner partner."

"I'm sorry? Yes. Yes, of course. Forgive me. Texas toothpicks for the wedding."

"No problem." Noah was staring at him oddly, but he didn't look mad.

"I'm sorry. Let me just text that to Trev, and then I'll be focused, I swear."

"You're tired. It's fine."

"I just want all the details taken care of for you."

"I do appreciate it." Those green eyes.

He needed to snap out of it. He was too tired. That was the only answer. He was just too tired.

Noah sat back in his chair and sipped his beer, back to the very picture of impersonality.

Mason felt very damned confused. What was wrong with him?

Why did he keep looking so hard?

Their food came soon enough, and Noah switched to iced tea.

"This calzone is the size of my head." Noah picked up the steak knife they'd brought with the big turnover.

"It's glorious. I should have gotten one, but burgers are easy."

"They are. I don't indulge like this too much. I'll be out at midnight running laps."

"You and me both. I haven't hit the gym in two weeks. The guys will think I'm dead."

They grinned at each other, another little commonality making it easier to sit and eat and chat.

"I can tell you're a gym guy. You're stacked to the ceiling."

"The ceiling's a ways off for me," he admitted. He was trying, though. He didn't have it in him to be all lean and willowy. He bulked up.

"It works for you. Trust me." That heat was back, the little flashes of it fascinating.

Speaking of heat, his cheeks were on fire. Just lit up like fireworks were exploding under his skin. He wasn't sure what to do, so he just chuckled. "Thanks. You too. I mean, whatever you do. Oh God."

Noah's eyebrow lifted up to his hairline. "Breathe. I promise not to bite."

"Shame."

A husky laugh was his reply. "You're way more fun than advertised, honey."

"Butthead." *You don't call your biggest client a butthead, Mason!*

"I kinda am. Used to getting my own way. Loud and Texan."

"Indeed. So tell me, why did you pick a tiny outfit like mine instead of one in Dallas?" They had to have a thousand contacts there, people they used.

"Sammy wanted the ranch up here. I tried to talk her into closer to home, but she had her heart set."

"You have to admit it's lovely, hmm?" Maybe not really made for a party this big, but lovely nonetheless.

"I love it. The mountains are so pretty."

"You should see them in the winter. It's majestic as anything."

"I might have to come back. Stoney tells me there's a hot tub." Noah waggled his eyebrows. That should have been cheesy as hell, but it wasn't.

"That is the rumor." Hell, he knew that not only was there a hot tub, but that Stoney and Ford had one that was private.

He loved the view they had from their little deck. Mason grinned, thinking how cold the Texan would probably find the mountains in the winter. His condo was right in the center of Aspen. Tiny, but you couldn't beat the location. He could walk everywhere, get coffee almost any time of day, and he knew all the locals, people and dogs.

"So are you a skier?" Noah asked, and Mason nodded.

"Sure. I love snowboarding best, but I do some downhill skiing."

"Snowboarding looks tough. I learned to ski on vacations to New Mexico when I was a teenager. I broke my ankle one year, and Momma never wanted to go back."

"Yeah, extreme sports are dangerous, but so's everything else. I bet you played some sort of ball in high school." Texans always did.

"I did. I was terrible at football, but I did it. I was good at baseball."

"Let me guess… third base."

"Yeah." Noah raised one eyebrow, a habit Mason noticed more and more. "How did you know?"

"You're too long-legged to be a catcher, and if you'd been a pitcher, you would have said so." Mostly it was a good guess.

"Well, that's better than 'third base is always the fat guy.' Which I've heard."

"Eh, they have to be able to pound it into home."

"We also have to be able to catch those line drives. I had one break my jaw in tenth grade. I was wired shut for weeks."

Ouch.

"That sounds awful. Only thing I've ever broken is a shoulder blade. You don't need those to eat."

"I bet that made for miserable sleeping, though." Noah leaned back and patted his belly. "Think I ought to get a box, or would that just offend Geoff?"

"Get a box. You have a microwave and a fridge in your room."

"Right. Good idea." Noah waved down their server, and they got the bill settled. They both groaned at the idea of dessert.

They headed out, gasping at the cold rain that splashed down on them. Freak summer storms like this always came before the more settled, daily rains of the so-called monsoon, and they always stung.

Noah unlocked the truck, and they hopped in, Noah getting the heater going. "It's June! Jesus, that's cold."

"Yeah. At least it's not snow." Down here, he thought. Up at the ranch, it wasn't impossible.

"Stoney and Ford said we might get some. I thought they were shitting me."

"No. Let's get a move on, huh? Are you comfortable driving?"

"I can do it, no worries."

The canyon would be fine, but once they turned up out of Glenwood toward the ranch, it could get hairy. They'd just have to see.

"Lead on, MacDuff."

They headed out, and for a while the rain let up, especially up around Island Acres. They hit it again at the end of DeBeque Canyon, though, and damned if it didn't start sleeting as they headed up toward the ranch.

Noah's hands were white-knuckled on the wheel, and Mason shook his head. This didn't work. It would be a shitty wedding if the bride's brother died in a car accident.

"You want to stop for the night? It's already taken more than an hour longer than it should, and my condo is ten minutes away."

"No shit?"

"Yeah. Just stay on this road into Aspen instead of turning up."

Noah nodded and blew out a breath. "Good deal. I appreciate it."

"No problem. I have coffee and whiskey and a gas fireplace." He'd let Noah have his bed, and he'd crash on the sofa.

"I like the sound of that. Who the heck has ice storms in June?"

"Welcome to the mountains. Okay, so we turn off here." Driving in town was way easier—the roads were better, and the city was on it. He got them parked in his little covered spot, doing his best to not notice the way Noah's hands shook.

The guy was probably used to tornados, but this kind of driving was an acquired skill, right?

Noah smiled, the lines around his eyes and mouth looking a little deep. "You said whiskey?"

"I did. Come on up. It's better when you're in and warm and relaxed."

He was on the third floor with this amazing view, the whole back of the condo glass. The place was tiny—TV, couch. The breakfast nook was his office, and the bedroom was mostly bed.

Noah followed him up, and it occurred to him he'd have to find something for the man to wear to bed, at least. Unless Noah slept naked. On his sheets. Oh man.

Stop it, Mason, you stupid perv.

Surely there was something….

Yeah, no. Noah had eight inches on him, easy, and it was all leg. The idea of Noah wearing his pajama pants was ludicrous. He could wash Noah's clothes, if need be.

"Lord. Cold." He could hear Noah's teeth chattering.

"Come in and settle by the fire." He had a remote and turned it on, grabbing a blanket off the back of the sofa. "Give me your shirt and I'll wash it. I know I have a sweatshirt that will fit you."

"Thanks." Noah stripped off his shirt, his chest and belly ripped with muscle, broad and hard.

Mason's lips went a little numb. *Hello.* He caught himself staring. "Sh-shirt, whiskey, and coffee. Be right back."

Oh fuck. Pretty. Genuinely pretty.

He was as shallow as the next guy sometimes. Mason took Noah's shirt so he could turn away, heading for his little stackable washer and dryer. He left the shirt and his own on the lid, then went to grab sweatshirts and warm socks.

Noah would just have to do a blanket or wet pants on the bottom.

"Are you a 'don't touch my coffeemaker' kind of guy?" Noah called.

"Not at all. K-Cups are in the cabinet right above."

"I'll fire it up, then."

He thought maybe Noah liked to feel useful. Mason understood. He hated perching on someone's couch and doing nothing.

Especially half-naked.

He did have a couple of sweatshirts that ought to work, plus socks, so he grabbed them and toed off his boots, texting Ford as he did.

Spending night in Aspen. All is well.

Getting snow here. People are tickled. Have Wright call sister.

Will do. We hit sleet.

Ack.

Yeah. See u 2morrow morning

Nite.

He tucked his phone into the pocket of his robe. "Ford says to call your sister. I'll take over the coffee making."

"Gotcha." Noah took the sweatshirt he offered, then tugged it on. Good thing he'd bought that one big to go over layers.

"I brought you some warm socks too. You want the whiskey on the rocks or in your coffee?" *Dear Mr. Wright, Would you be taken aback if I licked your belly? Yeah? Bummer. Disappointed but understanding, Me.*

"In the coffee is fine. Man, I ought to sleep like a rock. How do you drive in this shit?"

"Snow tires and chains. I grew up in Vail, man. I've never spent a winter anywhere else."

"Ah." Noah nodded. "I get it. People ask how we can stand floods and tornados. I mean, we get some snow in Dallas. A little ice. But in June? Shit."

"Yeah. I hear you. It's not too common, and it won't stick."

At least the family that was staying in the yurts weren't there yet….

"The weather is supposed to be perfect the day of the ceremony," Noah murmured. "Let me call Sammy."

"Sure. Sure, I'll be in with coffee. Sit by the fire."

"Thanks." He got a faint smile before Noah bundled up on his couch with a blanket, Noah's phone appearing out of nowhere, it seemed.

He started the laundry and made up the coffee, feeling a little like he was a stranger in his own house.

"Hey. No, we're fine. Yes, we got all your stuff. Seriously?" Noah's warm chuckle made him smile. "Okay. I heard. It was sleet down here, so we're going to. No. No, I will not. Night. Bye. Bye!"

"Here's your coffee. Is the fire helping?"

"It's great. Thanks. I like your place. It's wee, but everything has a function."

"I bought it for the view." And because he wanted to be on the top floor.

"Is it amazing?" Noah peered out his window. "I mean, it's kinda black right now."

"It's stunning." He headed over and pointed to the mass of black. "You see that? That's the mountains."

"That's too cool. Not much of a view in Dallas unless you mean the skyline." Noah set aside his phone. "There's a hum to it, though. A vibe."

"Sure. We're tiny here. It's a different world." Noah Wright had a plane, for God's sake. Planes. He had an SUV crossover and a one-bedroom apartment.

"It's not bad. Just so different." Noah leaned his head back and closed his eyes a moment. "This is weird. Not having anything to do."

Mason stood and changed the sheets for Noah, then sat at the desk, checking to see if Noah was awake or not.

"I really don't bite," Noah said, watching him. "You can come sit and watch the news or whatever."

"I was trying to let you rest." He was trying to be nice. "You look worn-out."

"So do you." Noah patted the seat next to him. "Come on, honey."

He walked over and sat beside Noah in a daze, the fire hypnotizing as it danced. He did love his little gas log. There was something primal about fire, even if the smell of woodsmoke had to come from his more distant neighbors.

"Did you get you a little shot of something yummy, Mason?"

"I did." And it was going right to his head.

"Yeah. Makes us better people, huh?" That drawl was so deep. Like slow-running molasses.

"That's the rumor. Makes things a little easier."

"Like lube."

He blinked. Click. "Yes, exactly. Emotional lube."
Don't laugh. Don't laugh.

Noah snorted, this truly rip-roaring sound, and they were off again, laughing just like they had in the truck in Grand Junction. He was leaning against Noah, almost howling with pure joy.

God, it felt good to let go and just wail with laughter. He thought it had been years.

"Damn, honey. When you let yourself laugh…." Noah looked at him like he was… hell, like he was worth staring at.

The laughter faded, and his cheeks heated again. It had to be the booze and the fire. Had to. All they needed was a fuzzy rug and it was a lead-in to a porno.

Boom chicka wow wow.

Christ.

Okay, get up, go to the bathroom. Put some space between you.

He half rose, pushing himself up on one arm, but Noah caught his free wrist, the momentum tugging him the rest of the way around. "Hey, I didn't mean to—"

His feet slipped out from underneath him, and his belly smacked against Noah's belly, pushing all his breath out of him.

"Oof." Noah caught his hips with both hands, and they stared at each other for a long moment. Then, just like in the movies, Noah pressed up to kiss him, their lips meeting warm and sweet. He took a deep breath, intending to pull back, back off, when Noah's tongue slid in between his lips, tasting him.

Mason gasped, melting into Noah a little. This was all wedding excitement. What harm could it do to bask in the attention for a minute?

Noah cupped the back of his head and pulled him in tight, groaning harshly as the kiss went deeper. One arm clamped around his back, not so hard he was worried, but definitely keeping him in place.

The man might not be into love, but he sure knew how to kiss, leaving Mason panting, his body on fire. His cock was heavy and full, his balls aching with a sudden need.

Noah pulled him up a little tighter, squeezing them together until he couldn't breathe.

They shifted to get a better angle on the kiss, their tongues tangling. Mason tried to hump a little, and that was when it all went terribly wrong.

Noah's grip slipped, and he dangled a moment before falling right into Noah's lap.

"Urgh." Noah grunted and shoved him off onto the floor with a thud.

He rattled a second, then blinked up from his spot. Okay. Ow. And also, what the ever-loving fuck was he thinking?

Kissing a client?

Fuck, he was a dipshit.

"Are you okay?" Hell, was he okay?

Noah looked down, his eyes actually watering. "Squashed my balls, man. Sorry I dumped you on the floor."

"No problem." He sat up and moved to the window, eyes searching the sky, and he fought for something to say that straddled the gap between "Oh my God, I'm sorry" and "Dude, you dropped me on the floor" and "Please don't fire me."

He settled on "Do you need an ice pack?"

"No." Noah shook his head, his smile rueful. "I'm okay if you are. I think I might sack out, though. Do you have a blanket for the couch?"

"I changed the sheets on the bed for you. Feel free."

"Hey, I can't put you out of your bed." Noah frowned a little. "This blanket will be fine. I, uh, don't guess you have an extra toothbrush?"

"I do. They come in threes, and the bed is yours. I fit on the sofa, after all."

"I—okay, but if you wake up with a crick in your neck, I didn't do it."

"Fair deal." If he woke up with a crick, he could go get a massage Saturday night.

"Thanks for today, Mason. I had a ball. So to speak." Noah rose, blanket around his waist.

"It was something else, absolutely. I'll put some towels and the extra toothbrush out in the bathroom for you."

"Thank you." Noah headed into the bedroom, leaving him and his once again flaming cheeks alone.

He put out the toiletries, poured another cup of coffee, then sat at his computer so he could log on to Skype. He had to know somebody who wanted to talk to the guy who couldn't do something right with detailed instructions.

Chapter Seven

THERE were two hundred people.

Noah felt a bit like a panicked horse. He hoped his eyes weren't rolling, but God. His baby sister was about to get married, and there were two hundred people.

"You ready, Daddy?" he asked.

"Yes, son. I'm ready for all this nonsense to be over so that Samantha can be home and settled."

"I know. She's so flighty." He winked at Doug's brother, who was still fiddling with his tie.

Bryan winked at him. "Are you going to dance with me at the reception, Noah? The media will all be gone by then…."

Right. Media. Mason had stood there with his teeth in his mouth when Sammy had informed them that she'd had her publicist in contact with a number of reporters and that they would need a place for them and all their equipment.

The man had dealt with it, but Mason had a visible tic now.

It sharpened every time Mason looked at his assistant, Trevor. Who had hooked up with Bryan….

"Uh, not this time, buddy. I'll leave that to the twink in the ruffles."

Bryan laughed, and Daddy and the other groomsmen snickered. Daddy had taken the proliferation of gayness pretty damned well. Stoney and him had become best buds and had done a lot of fishing.

"Mr. Wright, sir. I have Frank and his top hat here, sir." Quartz was dressed in his cowboy finery, the hat hiding the boy's eyes.

"Thank you, Quartz. I'll take him from here." He was reduced to leading the ring bearer into the service. Lord.

Sammy intended to ride in on one of the ranch's horses, and Noah was praying she didn't fall off into the dust.

They had Tanner as a wrangler, and Noah knew the man had been told that Sammy was pregnant. The whole ranch would be on alert.

"We're ready for Noah and Frank. Mr. Wright, sir? As soon as Sammy rides in, you'll meet her at the head of the carpet to walk her down the aisle." Mason was there, bustling, his radio in hand.

"You got it, kiddo." Daddy clapped Mason on the back. "You're three hours away from getting paid."

"Shh." Mason winked, but that tic popped a moment.

Noah owed the guy a bucket of whiskey.

"Come on, Frank. No farting."

Quartz laughed, following at a distance. He would wrangle Frank again when the ring part of the ceremony was over. Noah just had to get the drooly beast down the aisle without him eating the yellow rose petals the flower girls tossed.

Mason disappeared about the time Sammy showed.

THE ceremony itself was quick and simple, with a healthy dose of laughter and a few tears.

Just as a good wedding ought to be, he thought. Fast, funny, and meaningful.

The younger flower girl and Frank taking a moment to groom each other on the way down the aisle, complete with ear licking and shrieking giggles, made the whole thing complete.

When Brother Jeffries pronounced them man and wife, a cheer went up, and the world lit up with flashes.

Somewhere it had to be Miller time.

Quartz slid up beside him to take Frank, who was panting, stressed from the noise. "I'll take him somewhere quiet for a nap, sir."

"Good man. Thank you."

The photographer had taken pictures of Frank with Sammy and Doug earlier in the day. Also a good man.

After the endless family pictures, they swept into the reception with barely any time to breathe, arriving to a breathtaking array of nibbles.

The cake was easily five feet tall and covered in sugar bluebonnets and sunflowers, Indian paintbrushes and coneflowers. Stunning. Utterly magical.

"Oh, Noah, look." Momma had misty eyes, but she wore a big smile, and it felt good, knowing she was pleased. "Lovely. You did a fabulous job. I'm so proud of you."

He gave her a hug. "There's an amazing team here. Did you see these cameras? Take my picture!" He kinda felt like a kid again for a moment, giddy with relief that the whole thing had actually happened.

They were laughing and drinking, taking pictures and goofing off. It was amazing.

Then Sammy and Doug walked in, and it was better.

Sammy made the rounds, her dress short in front and long in back to show off her Lucchese boots. Her hair was sliding out of the bun her stylist had so painstakingly rolled, and she was five again in that instant, smiling at him with that little gap between her two front teeth.

"You happy, little girl?"

"Oh, Ark. Thank you. It's perfect!" She grabbed him, and he spun her around, catching sight of Mason out of the corner of his eye. The man had dark bags under his eyes that he could pack enough clothes for a three-week cruise in.

He'd done every damned thing the kids had asked and then some, and he was an amazing kisser on top of that. Kisses. He kissed Sammy's cheek. "I love you, baby girl. You be happy."

"I will. You arranged the surprise? In the car?"

"I did, just like you wanted."

"Smile!" Bryan snapped their picture with a Polaroid.

"Thank you. Okay, I'm off to cornhole with my husband!"

"Too much information!" He tugged off his jacket, because formal pictures were over. He grabbed a plate of tiny food before heading to the command center in the kitchen tent to see what he could do. Geoff had decided that was the best use of space.

He wanted to see Mason. The man had made him breakfast and coffee, then had been on the phone the whole drive up to the ranch. Since then, he hadn't been able to speak about that kiss, even once.

Noah figured maybe Mason thought that was fine, but he wanted…. Hell, what did he want? He wanted to get to know Mason better, at least.

"What are you doing in here, honey?" Geoff asked, laughing. "You are supposed to be celebrating!"

"I am! I'm not very good with that much crowd." He could be, if he had to, but he preferred not to deal with all the social niceties. "What can I do? I feel like a slug."

"Have you seen Mason? Has he collapsed somewhere?"

"I saw him just a few moments ago, running. Should I go sit on him?"

"Yes. It's about time Trev earned his keep." Geoff scowled, which he took to mean Trev was in trouble.

"Oh?"

"Yeah, he's been canoodling with the brother of the groom instead of applying himself."

"Got it." Canoodling. "The pigs in a blanket? Amazing."

"Thank you, sir. Want to know a secret?"

"You know I do."

"Vegan. All the way."

"You naughty man!"

Geoff looked pleased as punch. "I had to have something."

"You did. I saw that the pimento cheese finger sandwiches were gluten free. You're a genius." He clapped Geoff on the back. "Off to find Mason."

"Be nice to him, honey! He's about to crack down the center."

"I like him now, Geoff." Noah winked, but he found it was the truth.

Finding Mason was a bit like playing Marco Polo in an Olympic-size pool.

He finally found the man restocking the doughnut wall, covered in sugar up to his elbows.

"Hey." He joined Mason in the hanging. "When you're done here, can you tell Trev to take over a minute? I need a hand."

"I'll be right there." Mason nodded to him, almost managing a smile.

Noah chose to take that little curl of lips as a good sign.

They finished hanging doughnuts, and then Mason followed him to the groom's tent, which was empty now. He took Mason's hand so he could pull Mason over to the settee, where he tugged and pushed until Mason sat.

"Noah?" Mason blinked up at him, obviously confused.

"You need to sit for two minutes. Maybe have a snack."

"Oh. I'm not hungry, but thank you. Did you get some treats? It's still a bit before supper is served."

"I did. You need something, honey." He had the strongest urge to curl up with Mason and nap.

Mason blinked at him, and he reached out, tracing the shape of the man's nose, then his lips.

"What are you doing?" Mason asked.

"I have no idea. It seems good."

"You are something else."

Mason had no idea. He wanted to taste. And touch. And do things that were absolutely inappropriate.

"I just needed to see you," Noah said. "And you needed a minute to breathe."

"Are they enjoying themselves?"

"God, yes." He'd never seen so many hipsters and Dallas folks one generation away from rednecks have so damned much fun together.

Even the uppity Prestons seemed to be okay with it. How those stodgy folks had two sons with huge personalities and bigger senses of humor, he didn't know.

"Oh, good." Mason leaned over and rested their foreheads together. "I might sleep for a week."

"I know, honey. You've done so well. It's been amazing."

Mason's lips touched his. "This is a terrible idea, you know. You're a client."

"Shh. Only for a few more hours." And he didn't hold with all this nonsense. He'd made himself, and he'd kiss Mason if he wanted to.

"Oh. Huh." Mason sounded as if he'd never thought of that.

Noah grinned, because what else could he do? Mason needed a long soak in a tub, a nap, and a few dozen orgasms, not necessarily in that order.

He would be happy to provide the latter. He really would.

He took a kiss, moaning as it proved to be just as electric as the one they'd shared before. His head spun a little, and he wanted more. So much more.

Noah moaned, a deep, raw sound that poured from him and into Mason.

Mason started to crawl into Noah's lap, but a clearing of throat had them springing apart. *Damn it.*

"Guys. Seriously. The bride is hunting you, Mr. Noah, and Trev has disappeared, Mason. I need you, now." Stoney actually looked sorry to have interrupted.

"Crap." Mason sprang into action. "I will beat him to death."

"I might help," Stoney muttered.

"Thanks, Stoney." Noah rose as well, heading out to see what Sammy wanted.

This wasn't over, though.

Not by a long shot.

"Ark! You have to play before supper!" She tossed him a beanbag.

"Okay, okay." He hadn't taken a turn because he was wicked competitive and so was Sammy. They would get all serious.

"Come on, old man. Show me you're still a stud!"

"Old man!" He hooted with laughter before stepping up to the line so he could toss the beanbag. Hole in one. Who still had it?

"Why am I not surprised?" She walked up close and whispered, "Cornholer."

"That's me." He winked. "You interrupted my attempt."

She blinked at him innocently, but her false eyelashes killed the look.

"Yeah. I thought you wanted me to go for it."

"After the reception, okay?"

Noah nodded easily. "Deal."

"Thank you, Ark. Can you believe I'm married? Me? For reals?"

"No." For a moment, he wanted to snatch her up and run. She'd been his responsibility for so long, his little sister. "Now you're Doug's problem, huh?"

"Like I don't need you. You're my Ark, rain or shine."

"I am." He kissed the top of her head. "Now, who's up for a doughnut?"

"Hrm. Dinner's going to be pretty damn yummy. Want to share one with me?"

"I do." He had no idea if he did or not, but that would get them away from cornholing for sure.

She leaned into his arm. "Daddy bought me a house—that custom that backs onto your property. We're going to be neighbors."

"Yay?" Oh, Lord. There would be four-wheeling and bonfires and constant cookouts. Maybe he needed to get a loft in the city.

"No?" She blinked up at him. "I'll tell him we changed our minds. I thought you'd be excited."

"I am." He was just stupid tired. "Shit, I get to have you, and you know who else." Noah winked. "I'm tickled, baby girl."

"Yeah? Because we can't wait to have you over. Besides, I can keep an eye on you and the 'rents."

"And keep an eye on my place when I'm traveling. Is that bacon and maple?"

"Mmm. My favorite." She pulled it off the board and tore it in half.

The crowd about them hooted and hollered, the sound pure Texan, through and through.

Sammy flexed, spinning around in her fancy dress like a monkey.

Noah laughed when Doug came to dance her away, catching her midspin. They looked so good together. So happy. He just loved her so much, and he was so damned proud.

"They're silly kids, huh?" Daddy grabbed a doughnut, his chocolate cherry.

"They are. Was I ever that young?" He didn't think so. Life had been very different when he was a teenager and young adult.

"No, son. You were born thirty."

"I thought so." He nudged his daddy with his elbow. "You still having a good time?"

"Well, I'd rather be fishing." Daddy winked at him.

"You have to dance with Sammy, and then you're excused from the drama and can go fishing tomorrow."

"I intend to. Someone is taking your momma shopping in Aspen. She's tickled as a pig in shit."

"Good deal. Did Sammy figure something for the dog?"

"Yeah. Your cousin Martha is taking him back with her and her son."

"Good deal. I sure would hate to make the old feller fly. He'd gas himself to death." Noah chuckled. "Maybe I ought to get a dog."

"You're good enough with animals." Daddy winked, bumped their shoulders together. "You work with all them financial folks, after all."

"All so you can go fishing." He jerked his chin toward the dance floor. "I think it might be time for food." The waiters were all filing in and standing about, looking ready.

"Ah. We have to sit and eat, then. We have place cards and everything. You said there was going to be decent barbecue?"

"You're gonna think they brought up a Texas pit master." He would prep Daddy to like it, and he would.

"It smells okay. I do like a plate of meat." Daddy looked around. "Where is your momma? She'll have to come eat with us."

"I'll go find her." Noah spent the next ten minutes running to track people down, until he heard Stoney ringing the big triangle grub bell.

He hoped Mason had found himself a bite to eat.

Trev was there, changed out of the ridiculous ruffled tux and into a black shirt and tie. He directed traffic like a pro, so at some point he must have been a waiter himself.

Bryan was there too, fluttering around Trev, teasing and distracting.

Oh, this was about Sammy and Doug. Not the best man and the… Trev.

Noah was about to go have a word, when Mason swept through, taking Trev off with him. The leaving caused just the barest ripple, but he had a feeling Trev was getting reamed.

They sat, and he made himself focus. Sammy. Food. Dancing. Cake. This was her day. It would be gone soon enough. He needed to pay attention to this.

Not the wedding planner.

Not the pretty, stacked little wedding planner.

Chapter Eight

MASON watched the bride and groom drive off, the look on Doug's face almost as good as all the family's.

He headed for the kitchen and ended up sitting on the steps of the porch in the dark, wishing he had a cigarette or a joint or a french fry. Any one would do.

He'd done it. He'd really pulled it off. He was under budget, on time, and he felt like the bride and groom believed it had been perfect.

It hadn't been, of course. He'd had to run to Aspen twice, he owed a metric fuckton of favors, and he was fairly sure he was going to die, but that was his to know.

The door opened behind him, and someone tried to run him down, both of them oofing hard. "Shit. Mason? Is that you?" Geoff reached to help him stand, since he'd toppled like a bowling pin.

"Sorry. Sorry." Maybe he'd just stay here. The ground wasn't that hard.

"Come in, Mason. I've got Ford and the dogs, but that's it. It's warm and quiet."

"Uh-huh." He forced himself to move, to get up to hands and knees. He could do this. He knew how.

Geoff helped lift him. "Oh, Noah, hey. Help Mason inside? I think he's whipped."

Noah swept up the stairs, lending him a strong arm, and Geoff went off to do whatever it was he was leaving the house to do.

"I'm sorry. I'm okay." He wasn't okay. Not even a little.

"No, you're exhausted."

Ford sprang up when they walked in, moving to pull out a chair for him. Noah lowered him to it gently.

"What would you like to drink, Mason?" Ford asked.

"Can I have a Coke, please?" Bubbles, sugar, and caffeine—the magic triangle.

"Quartz?"

"Yessir." Quartz hopped up, moving to grab a Coke from the fridge. Frank, who was under the table, rolled over to lie on Mason's feet, then burped.

He began to chuckle, and then the laughter got louder, almost tearing out of his belly.

Ford patted his arm, grinning like a loon, while Noah sat down next to him, nudging him with the nearest elbow. "That's his whole opinion."

"Indeed. She seemed happy. I was afraid your mom was going to pass out when she saw the getaway car."

"Pass out? Shit, I thought she was fixin' to stroke out." Stoney wandered through with a bus tub of dessert plates.

"Let me help—"

"No!" Ford and Noah said it in concert, both of them holding him down with a hand on his arm.

"This is Stoney's last load," Ford said rather sternly. "We have a pair of dishwashers to do that."

"I was heading in, so I grabbed it. I'm fixin' to have a beer to celebrate. Who wants to join me?"

"Mr. Mason wanted a Coke, Daddy."

"I think he probably needs that more than a beer, kiddo. Why don't you have a little can of Sprite with him so he doesn't feel alone?"

"Yes, sir."

There was something about Quartz, this way of seeing things, that Mason appreciated.

"Thank you, Quartz, and thank you for keeping such good track of Frank. Sammy was so happy he was here."

Quartz nodded to him, not so much as cracking a smile. "You have to take care of those that depend on you. Stewardship is what it's called."

"Yes, sir. That's absolutely right," Mason said.

"He makes a good foot warmer," Noah murmured.

"Frank?" Mason glanced down at the freckled belly turned up to him. "He does."

"Even if his name should be Frankenfarter," Ford said.

Quartz blinked and then started giggling, the sound surprisingly young and infectious, so Mason started laughing along.

When Geoff came in with a giant hotel pan full of leftovers, he found them all hooting, Janie the border collie looking from one to the other of them and whining.

"What did I miss?" Geoff asked, setting them all off again.

"Fart joke," Stoney said. "Beer?"

"Heck yes." Geoff slid the pan onto the counter. "This is for our fridge if you guys want anything. I was thinking of tossing some fries in the air fryer and making grilled cheese."

"Yes, please. That sounds heavenly." The words were out before he even knew he was speaking.

"I thought so." Geoff perked right up, which made them all exchange smiles. The man was never too tired to feed someone. Never.

Mason sipped his Coke and watched Geoff cook, letting the conversation ebb and flow around him. Noah's deep Texas drawl was a strange kind of comfort. He could listen to that all the time.

He let himself have a little fantasy. What if he'd met Noah on the street in Aspen? Just a random meeting of two men. Would Noah have gone to coffee with him? Would Noah have come up to his condo and admired the view?

Did it matter?

He was fascinated by the casual billionaire, by this man who drove him to Grand Junction instead of snapping his fingers and having an assistant do it.

Mason thought he might have dozed off while he waited. The warm press of a hand around his woke him, and he glanced over to find Noah holding his hand.

"You're okay, honey."

"Oh good." He wanted to be okay.

"Voila." Geoff presented him with a Texas toast grilled cheese and a side of fries with little bowls of ketchup and mustard.

"It smells like heaven. Thank you." He stared at the food, watching the steam rise.

"You want me to cut it in half?" Noah asked quietly.

Mason got the impression Noah knew what it felt like to be too tired to face a whole sandwich.

Don't nod. Don't nod. Had he just nodded? Out loud?

"Here." Noah cut his sandwich into fingers, four of them, and that he could cope with.

It really did taste like heaven too. Rich and cheesy and buttery. He approved.

Every bite perked him up a little bit, and by the time he was finished, he could think again.

"So we did hire a cleaning crew, right?"

"We did," Ford agreed. "They have their instructions, and Trev offered to stay late and make sure the food was all put away safely, at least."

"What are you going to do with all the leftovers?" Noah nibbled a piece of wedding cake, because Geoff had brought an entire layer in.

"Feed everyone tomorrow. Feed the drovers. I'll send a good chunk to Angie's house too. Freeze brisket." Geoff grinned at Noah, winked. "I can make you a to-go box for Monday."

"Any of the canned stuff or frozen stuff we don't eat can go to the Feed My Sheep shelter in Glenwood." Stoney shrugged when Geoff stared. "I know it's near and dear, buddy."

"My hero." Geoff kissed Stoney's cheek playfully, then did it again when Ford growled.

"Geoff, Daddy is taken." Quartz yawned. "May I be excused? I want to take Frank out one more time before we go to bed."

"I love that," Noah whispered, and Mason glanced up.

"What's that?"

"That no one cares, you know? That they're just a family."

Mason nodded, although he was sure he didn't understand. This was a special place, a safe spot no matter what.

"It's magical here" was all he said.

Frank rolled to his feet, rising at some unseen sign from Quartz.

"It is." Noah took his hand again and held on.

He sat there, his entire focus on that spot where his palm touched Noah's. Noah's hand was dry, smooth, warm.

Mason thought he hadn't blushed this much in his life. Not since high school. When Geoff smiled at him, looking a little misty, he wanted to say it was nothing, that Noah was just a client.

It wasn't true, but he wanted to say it.

"Okay, y'all. I don't know about you, but I'm fixin' to fall over. We'll do whatever's left in the morning, huh?" Stoney smiled at Noah, rolling his eyes. "Not you, of course, Mr. Noah. You're our guest."

"I can throw in to help if I need to." Noah rose but never let go of Mason. "Can I walk you to your room? I just need a few moments."

"Of course. Yes. Good night, guys. Good night." He followed, feeling a little dazed and confused.

They got to the guest room where he'd set up his little command center. Noah led him inside, and he moved right to the bed to sit. "Sorry. I'm feeling better since the food, but I'm pooped."

"I understand." Noah grabbed a chair and sat across from him.

"Hi."

Noah smiled. "Hi. Thank you. For Sammy's wedding."

"Was she happy?" Because really, that was why he did it. One day of magic.

"Over the moon. Even the mother of the groom had fun." Noah paused, hands linked loosely in front of him. "The wedding is over, though. I'm not a client anymore."

"No. No, you're not." He swallowed, eyes locked with Noah's.

"I know we're both a little loopy, but I really want to kiss you again, Mason." Noah didn't sound a bit businesslike. Not a bit.

"I haven't had a drop of booze, Mr. Wright. Not one drop." He leaned in and brought their lips together, breathing Noah in, filling his lungs with Noah's air.

"Good." Noah pressed in close, the kiss long and slow, heating up gradually. He found Noah's thighs, the crease in the starched jeans fascinating his fingers.

Noah slid from the chair to the bed, turning him so they damn near bumped noses. No dumping him on the floor this time.

"Hello, Mr. Wright." He moaned, the kisses heady, making his world spin.

"You taste so good. I want to touch you." So polite, so sweet, so seductive.

"Please. You're so fine." Go him with the erotic pillow talk.

Noah pushed him down gently, lying next to him so they were face-to-face. Laughing, they scooted up toward the headboard so their feet stopped dangling.

"We should have taken your boots off first," he teased.

Noah turned pink but shot back with "And your ass is sitting in a pile of gingham ribbons."

"Excellent point."

As one, they both rolled off the bed. Noah kicked out of his boots, and Mason swept aside the comforter, taking off all the wedding detritus. Better.

"Are we going to admit that we're fixin' to sleep together tonight, honey?" Noah asked.

"We are." Never let it be said Mason didn't throw himself wholeheartedly into his mistakes.

"Good." Noah began to undress, and Mason let himself watch a little bit, admiring the long, lean lines, before he stripped off his filthy T-shirt, shocked at the moan that filled the air.

Noah stared at him, eyes bright with desire. "I knew you'd be ripped under there."

He flexed—not because he was showing off, but because a wave of need hit him like an avalanche. He panted with it, fumbling with his button and zipper. He needed a shower, but he thought Noah did as well, so they were even.

He crawled up into the bed, Noah following him down and reaching for him before he was even horizontal. The first touch they shared, skin to skin, stole his breath and whatever good sense he had left.

Noah put one hand on his hip, thumb rubbing against his skin. The other hand rested on his chest, right over his heart, and Noah's kiss made him dizzy again.

He let one leg slide up between Noah's thighs, bringing their cocks close enough to rub, get that breath of friction.

"Uhn." Noah jumped a tiny bit, hips rocking.

Lord, someone was hot off the mark. He appreciated the thought—his balls ached with wanting this fine man.

"I need to know." He reached down, measured Noah from base to tip, learning the entire length of Noah's hard shaft.

Perfect. Long and hard, just thick enough to really create some weight against his palm…. Mason wanted all sorts of things to happen with that cock.

"Please, honey. Please. Your touch." Noah wiggled, trying to get more.

"You're hot as hell and twice as hard." He stroked up and down, then scooted even closer so he could reach down with both hands.

Noah stared at him, dark green eyes focused on him like a snake's. Or a rabbit's. Something. Whatever.

Maybe not the sexiest images. That focus was intense. Better.

"Hand stopping. Why?" Noah's little smile teetered on the edge of uncertain.

"I was caught in your eyes." Was that stupid? He started stroking again, because that would make it not matter.

"I can live with that answer." Noah snagged his mouth in another kiss, and there was nothing slow burn about this one. It was a full-out attack on Mason's senses. He fought to keep moving, to find that rhythm that he could stick with, something natural and easy. Otherwise he'd get lost in this kiss again.

Noah reached around to grip his ass, squeezing with both hands. That little roughness made Mason's toes curl. He couldn't believe they were doing this, couldn't fathom how good it felt.

Everything in his vision, in all his senses, was Noah.

He squeezed tighter, thumbs working the slick tip of Noah's cock on the next upstroke. Noah grunted, dragging them together, trapping his hands between them.

They rolled, Noah on top of him, and he had to let go so he could reach up and grip Noah's shoulders. They rocked, their cocks rubbing together hard, the friction almost unbearable. They were roaring along now.

He managed to get one leg wrapped around Noah's ass, making it just that much better.

"Uh-huh. Faster." Noah stared down at him, cheeks burning, lips parted.

"Faster." He was totally into that. Completely and utterly. "Come on. Need you."

Like he needed his next breath.

"Yeah." Noah drove down against him, pushing him. They needed this too badly to slow down, to try to make it last. Mason didn't want to think about only doing this once, but even if this was it, it felt too good, too right. "Come on, honey, give it up."

Yeah. Yeah, give all of it.

Noah kissed him one last time, which was all it took. That tiny, stinging bite to his lower lip sent Mason over the edge, and he cried out into Noah's mouth when he shot, hot and wet between their bellies.

Noah followed along in short order, driving against him with quick, brutal strokes. The expression on Noah's face was fierce, damn near feral. One of pure need.

Mason held him, his heart still racing, his body shaking a little. Damn. Just damn.

"I got you." Noah held him close, rocking him. "I got you, honey. Breathe."

"I forget how."

"I hear you." Noah laughed, the sound a wee bit shaky. "Wow."

His own chuckles joined with Noah's, low and close to hysterical. Frankly, Mason wasn't sure how much more his body could take.

"Do you need to hit the bathroom, honey?" Noah asked, not letting him go one bit.

"No. I think I'll just stay right here. Possibly forever."

"I think that sounds like a great idea." Noah shifted to the side some to give him some air, that big body going a little boneless. "Long day."

"Yes." But it was over, and it had been successful.

Both those things were good.

Not as good as the man resting against him, maybe, but pretty damn good, nonetheless.

He smiled up at the ceiling for a moment, so proud of their team, his hands moving gently on Noah's back.

Then Mason closed his eyes, and that was all it took to put him right to sleep.

Chapter Nine

BREAKFAST was amazing, and the mountain air cleared whatever fog was still in Noah's head from the previous day. He sat with his coffee out on the makeshift patio that had been set up for the wedding party, and damned if Noah couldn't stop grinning.

Especially when he got to watch Mason bustle back and forth, making sure the cleanup crew had done their job.

Now that he'd had that muscled butt in his hands, he couldn't stop looking at it. Lusting after it either. He had to watch his step or he'd end up making trouble for Mason, at least while the wedding party was still mostly here.

Momma was in Aspen, getting her shopping on. Daddy had gone out with Tanner at first light to fish. There were still a lot of folks milling about, though.

"Pardon me, Mr. Wright?" Doug's father wore a pair of slacks and a golf shirt, and he looked decidedly uncomfortable. Noah wasn't sure why the man would have come back to the ranch from Aspen when there was a plane waiting for them there.

"Mr. Preston." He never felt good calling the man Terry.

"I don't suppose you have seen the young man that runs the event planning? I'm afraid we are going to have words."

Christ. Dallas royalty could suck his left nut.

"Why is that, sir?" Noah sat up straight, knowing he was more intimidating when he appeared formal rather than relaxed.

"His gold-digging tramp of an assistant has run off with my son!" Preston hissed. "Can you imagine? I want an apology, I want the man fired, and I want a refund for your expenses!"

"For my expenses?" He blinked. "I'm not sure I understand."

"For this… this nonsense! Cabins and mason jars and a hound dog for a ring bearer? This is going to be on the society page! And now? Someone has seduced my son!"

Oh, no one had seduced Bryan Preston. Bryan had been stalking Trev on sight. It had been funny as fuck, barring the whole thing where Mason had had to work twice as hard.

Noah took a deep breath. "Your son, the one who got married, I mean, approved all of this. Well, maybe not the seduction, but he was the one who insisted on cornholing and the doughnut wall."

"Yes, well, we were hoping that Samantha would curtail some of this nonsense, not encourage it."

"You have met my sister, right?" He chuckled, trying to lighten the mood. "Are you happy about the news? You're going to be a grandpa."

"We would have been happier if they'd waited until after their honeymoon to catch, but yes."

Wow. Okay. Noah shrugged. "Things happen as they do. I'm sorry you were unhappy with the accommodations and the ceremony, but Sammy was pleased, and Doug seemed pretty good with it."

"Still, I need to speak with someone regarding the current unpleasantness."

"You mean with Bryan? Why don't you speak to him if you're so worried about your son fucking the help?" It popped out because he was getting pretty damned pissed.

"Excuse me? Vulgarity is the sign of an uneducated mind."

"Is there a problem, Mr. Preston?" Mason stood there, pale but calm, the only sign of distress the glitter in those blue eyes.

"There is. Your employee has absconded with my son!"

Mason didn't react, just answered calmly. "Has he? Well, the event is over, Mr. Preston. What Trevor does in his time off is not my affair, I'm afraid."

"He seduced my son! They left together last night."

"I wish them much happiness."

"I want him fired!" Preston bellowed, and Mason didn't so much as flinch.

"That isn't possible, sir. Trevor tendered his resignation last night."

Noah fought the urge to laugh out loud. Looked like Trev was hoping to become a kept man.

Given how Doug had fallen for Sammy and never once let her doubt it, he wasn't sure Trev wasn't lucky.

"Well, I—" Preston sputtered and waved his hands.

"Do you need a ride back to Aspen?" Noah asked. "I think perhaps you ought to head on out."

"You owe this man his money back! I will tell everyone about this."

"About how your son seduced my assistant and left me high and dry?"

Oh, there was that temper.

Preston took a step back. "I beg your pardon?"

"It will take me months of costly training to replace Trevor. Not to mention the hours of work it will take me to change passwords and bank records and such. I should invoice Bryan."

Man, Mason was in high dudgeon. Noah had read that term in a book when he was a kid, and he adored the turn of phrase.

"This wedding was arranged exactly as per instruction. The bride and groom both expressed their approval, as did the man bankrolling the ceremony. I appreciate that you're unhappy that your son's queer, but honestly, that's outside my purview. I just do weddings, not matchmaking."

"I—well, I…."

"No." Noah slapped his hand down on the table, then stood. "That's enough, Mr. Preston. I'm sorry you're not pleased. However, I paid for this damned wedding, and I am perfectly happy with both Rustic Romance and the Leanin' N. Do you understand?"

"I'm going to speak to my son about this!"

"When you do, tell Trev to send me back my keys. He forgot."

Preston stormed off, shoulders hunched and fists clenched.

"That is one pissed-off man," Noah murmured.

"He needs to remove the stick from out of his ass. He'd feel better."

"He totally would." He glanced at Mason. "Trev really quit on you?"

"He's heading to Maui with Bryan."

"Wowie." When Mason glared, he chuckled. "Okay, that was stupid, but it popped out. I'm sorry, honey."

"It's okay. I just have to hire someone else." Mason sighed, looked around. There were cowboys dismantling yurts, someone filling ditches from where the semi had left the fancy-assed port-a-potties, and a handful of bridesmaids riding horses in the pasture. "This was a wedding like no other."

"It sure was unique." He caught Mason's hand with his. "You all right?"

"I'm okay. I think. I've never… not with a client."

"No?" Noah had to admit, that was truly cool. That he was the one to tempt Mason into it. "I'm glad you did."

"I am too."

"Are you?" He searched Mason's face, wanting to see something there. Noah wasn't sure what.

"Yeah. I mean…." Mason shrugged. "Yeah."

"Thank you." He smiled because he had to. "I'm sorry he's such an old fusspot."

"Fusspot. Man, you can tell you two are related now…."

"I was trying to be nice." Noah winked. "What all else do you have to do today?"

"To be honest, I was going to rest for a day or three, but Trev…."

"Oh, man. You have an event midweek. Is there anything I can do to help?" He would have to go home soon, get back to his own business, but he wanted to steal more time with Mason.

"Tell me you aren't flying out tonight?"

"Nope. Day after tomorrow." He crossed his fingers to cover the lie, because as soon as Mason turned his back, Noah would text Maydell and have her arrange it.

"You have plans?"

"I don't." Noah made a surprise face. "I kinda rearranged my schedule when I figured out how much I liked it up here."

"I'd rearrange my plans for you, Mr. Wright."

Noah melted. Just pure-D melted. "Would you? How about dinner tonight?" Even if they stayed and let Geoff cook for them, it would be magical.

"How about dinner and a nooner?"

"I can totally get behind that." He took Mason's hand so they could go wherever they were going together.

Chapter Ten

THEY ended up staying at the ranch for the day. Stoney took Mason's phone, and Mason went to pretend that he didn't have problems and clients waiting for him, that Noah wasn't a billionaire with more power and personality and wealth than he'd ever have, and they went to have a picnic up in the mountains, complete with basket, blanket, and beer.

They sat together after they ate the fried chicken and coleslaw and potato salad Geoff made for them, holding hands and playing twenty questions about each other's life.

"You seriously were in a motorcycle gang?" Mason stared over at Noah, wide-eyed. "That's either cool or terrifying."

"I know, right? My wild days are long over." That quirky little smile on Noah's lips told Mason the man was pretty proud of his past.

"I'm not wild. I grew up in Denver, went to Colorado State, got a job in Aspen, and have been here ever since."

"We were dirt poor when I was little, but then Daddy found a business he could do, and we moved up slow but sure until I struck oil." Noah picked at a bunch of grapes. "Now I work all the time. Does that sound whiny?"

"No. It seems like that way. The more successful you are, the crazier life gets. I mean, I'm not successful like you are, but I get it on the small scale."

"You run yourself ragged. You did say you hadn't done anything on the scale of Sammy's wedding before, but I was damned impressed." Noah reached out to touch the back of his hand. "I didn't want to be at first."

"We're supposed to be prissy assholes. That's why I do rustic, outdoor living, and redneck events. It suits my personality."

"It sure does." Noah touched his wrist, then slid long, strong fingers up his arm. "I expected you to be more flamey, really."

"I feel like I am here sometimes, but I am who I am." And he sort of liked it, to be honest.

"That's a good thing." Noah moved a little closer.

"Is it?" He plucked a grape and reached to slide it over Noah's bottom lip.

"It is. You're strong and organized, hot as hell, and willing to go toe-to-toe with me and Old Man Preston. I need someone who can tell me to go to hell." Noah nipped the grape out of his hand.

"I wish you weren't going home so soon. I mean, I'm not asking you to stay. I'm not stupid. I have clients, you have a vast corporation deal, and we both have to work, but still, I'll miss you." Listen to him, spilling his guts like a dork. He was having a summer fling.

"Me too. I—" For a confident, übersuccessful man, Noah could sure evince uncertainty. "I want to see you again, Mason. For real."

"Yes." Simple as that. Yes. He reached out, then moved to straddle Noah's thighs. "I think we have something, Noah."

"I think we do too. Kiss me?" Noah held him in place, hands on his hips.

"I can do that." He leaned forward, the ease of this still making shivers slide down his spine. He'd had many new lovers over the years, and they had all taken more work. Even if they'd never dumped him on the floor.

The kiss started out nice and slow, and he reminded himself that ticks in delicate places—hell, ticks in any places—were bad. They would just have to make out like fiends and save the acrobatics for an indoor romp.

"You think all the time, O'Reilly. All the time."

"It's my job."

"I'm not a client here. I'm a lover."

Right. Noah's words made him melt again.

"Mmm. Much better." Noah grabbed him, fingers digging into his scalp, and he groaned, licking into Noah's mouth.

They were going to set the woods on fire.

Chapter Eleven

"MAYDELL, I need those soil sample reports." Noah was about to head out of the office for the day, and he was already stripping off his tie and jacket. The early July heat out there was brutal, and he would be drenched with sweat before he even made it to his SUV.

"You got it, honey. Seriously, you're as sore as a bear with a bee sting."

"Sorry, lady. I don't mean to be." Two weeks. It had been just over two weeks since he'd seen Mason, and while they texted a lot, neither of them had time to call or skype too much.

Noah missed his lover.

Which was stupid. He'd had long-distance love affairs before, for fuck's sake. He'd had this little hard body in London…. Damn.

Mason was different. Mason made him want to be there, to share space. He'd learned more about Mason in one afternoon than he'd known about Geordie from London in six months.

He wanted to fly himself up to Aspen and see that amazing view from that small but lovely condo and then kiss Mason into stupidity.

Kiss among other things.

Maybe he would. He could go for the weekend. One meeting Friday morning he couldn't blow off, but then he could file that flight plan....

He grabbed his phone and nodded to his driver, Bill, mouthing "Home." Then he called Mason.

"Hey, honey. What's up? No, Rachel. Don't file my emails. Don't *touch* my emails."

"Hey, darlin'. I was thinking I could come up this weekend. In Friday night, out Sunday morning?"

"I'll be in Denver all weekend working the Colorado Cattleman's Association annual meeting, Mister. You know weekends are deadly for me, especially in the summer."

"Yeah." Damn. "I was just hoping to slide in. How are you?" Mason sounded harried, and Noah hated to add to stress. "Should I call back tonight?"

"No, I'm going to sit in my office and talk to you and not fire my new assistant."

"Have you heard from Trev?"

"I got my keys in the mail."

"Oh, man." Noah winced. Bryan was still in Hawaii, so he guessed Trev was as well. Living it up. "Well, I have a driver today, and there's hellacious traffic. I can chat."

"Oh good. I'm dreading the traffic in Denver. That's why I'm going in Thursday and leaving as soon as possible Sunday."

"I bet. It's a bear here." Maybe Sunday. If Mason got home by noon….

"What are you doing for dinner?" He loved how Mason wanted to know the minutiae of his life.

"Probably ordering Chinese. I can take it tomorrow for lunch." He suddenly missed Geoff's heavenly cooking too. He ate a lot of crap.

"I have a sandwich in here. Could be turkey, could be roast beef."

Oh. Oh, that didn't work for him. He grabbed his tablet and started searching for a restaurant that would deliver. He knew Mason liked a barbecue place and a pho place that both delivered.

Boom. The Hickory House would do it.

"Don't eat a mystery sandwich, honey."

"I don't have time to go out, love. It won't kill me."

"No, there's a better meal on its way." Potato wedges and pickles. Mason would love it. "Maybe I should stop on the way home and get barbecue."

"Mmm. Barbecue. I want to come to Texas someday and try the barbecue there."

"But the Hickory House will have to do for today."

"You did not." Mason laughed, sounding delighted. "You rich bitch."

"What? I just ordered online. Anyone can do that."

"You spoil me."

Lord, if Mason felt that was spoiling, Noah couldn't wait to show him. He had a wealth of spoiling techniques at his fingertips.

"I need you to think of me fondly, honey."

"I always do, Mister. Always." Mason sighed. "Man, I miss you."

"Me too, honey. Like a sore tooth."

"Why do people say that?" Mason chuckled warmly. "I mean I know it means like you keep poking at the tooth with your tongue or whatever, but ow."

"Dork." He looked at filing flight plans and at commercial flights on his tablet, and Sunday just wasn't going to happen. *Damn it.* He sighed softly. "Can you skype tonight? I want to see you."

"Only if you can wait up late. I'll be at a cocktail charity event until ten, and cleanup will take me until eleven. That's why I'm locked in here now talking to you." Mason hummed, which meant he was thinking. "FaceTime?"

"God yes." He opened the program and called, smiling as his own personal little gym bunny appeared.

"Hey, Mister." Mason blew him a kiss.

"Oh, that's better. Hi." Noah smiled so hard his cheeks hurt.

"You're still hot as hell."

"It's been a couple weeks." He had no idea why he said that.

"It's been twenty-three days."

"Has it?" Oh, Mason was keeping track. Woo and hoo. That was seriously good.

"Yes. I know, I'm a dipshit, but… I know."

"I have it on my calendar but not in my head." He circled each day in red. Maydell thought he'd lost his mind. "So, what should we do on our next date?"

Mason looked at him, one eyebrow lifting as he got this wicked, knowing look.

"Well, that too. But last time we did a picnic first."

"That was fun, hmm? How do you feel about hot springs?"

"Pretty positive, though the pool in Glenwood isn't very private."

"No, I was thinking a trip to Orvis."

"Orvis?" That was one he didn't know.

"Up near Ouray. Private spa rooms. Hot springs water."

"Private spa rooms, hmm?" Oh, that had possibilities.

"Very clean. Clothing optional."

"How often do you go, then?" Not that he was a jealous guy. Not at all.

"Look, Mister. I was never in a motorcycle gang. Let me have my clothing optionalness."

"You went on a dare, didn't you?"

Oh, look at that blush.

"You totally did!" Noah fist-pumped the hand not holding the phone. "Trevor?"

"No. No, my best friend and his husband. They're turds."

"Ah." Noah nodded sagely. "You went to see them, right?"

"Yes, my goddaughter's birthday." Mason grinned, obviously surprised. "How on earth did you know that?"

"I was calling that weekend to try to get the menu changed for the rehearsal dinner. I might have pestered Trev half to death."

"And you never once mentioned that Sammy was a girl."

"No. I assumed you knew, and frankly, Trev and I didn't speak the same language. He just kept saying if I wanted any changes, I would have to speak to you on Monday." How they'd skated through the whole lead-up to the wedding without Mason knowing Sammy was a girl still mystified him.

It impressed him too, that Mason dealt with it well enough that Sammy didn't even know.

"Trev had his moments, but I swear, I can't cope with this training shit. I've done every event since you left essentially on my own."

"Oh, honey, you've got to be exhausted."

"Like you don't work your ass off."

"I have Maydell. Despite her lack of telling you there was a bride and groom, she and I are a well-oiled machine." He dreaded her retirement.

"Well, then, make sure you don't introduce her to anyone that's going to take her to Hawaii."

"Right." He would make a note.

"How are Sammy and Doug? Are they back yet?"

"They are. They're staying in my guesthouse while they renovate their place. We already have two horses and a donkey in addition to Frank."

"I can't believe I brought you to my condo. Your guesthouse is four times the size."

"I love your condo." He did. The view was amazing, and the place was totally Mason. "The bed is great."

"I didn't sleep that whole night, you know? After you kissed me."

"Don't you mean dropped you on the floor?"

"That too." Mason's chuckle was warm. Intimate. "You were the first guy to ever do that as well. To be fair, you had squished balls."

His knees drew up at the memory of that deep ache, even now. "Yeah. I damn near puked."

"I'm sorry." Mason pulled the best face, all sorrow mixed with laughter.

"Hey, it was worth it to have what I have now." Which was still not enough, damn it. "What are you doing next Tuesday night?"

"Next Tuesday night? Why?"

"Well, I can't come up, but if we make a date, we can skype dinner together. We can have pasta and salad. Deal?" Weeknights were better for Mason, usually.

"God, you're…. Yes. I'd love that. My romantic Texan."

"That's me. Delicate. Sensitive. Pasta from a can doesn't count, but freezer bags with those little chunks of frozen sauce totally do."

"Like you eat pasta from a can."

Well, no. He had staff. If he wanted pasta, Hank made him pasta. Still, he knew Mason would cheat, given the opportunity. He'd seen the Chef Boyardee. Though, maybe that was for the goddaughter when she visited.

"Hell, pick up something on the way home, honey."

"I will figure something out. I'll put you on my calendar."

He smiled for Mason, tickled as hell. If he went on the calendar, it was set in stone. "You tell me what time."

Mason typed on his computer for a second. "Let's see…. Seven my time, eight yours?"

"Sounds great." That was doable even if he hit traffic or had to have something delivered.

Mason sighed, lashes shadowing his eyes for a moment. "My food is here. Thank you. I have just enough time to eat and change before the event setup."

"Go on and eat in peace, then. I miss you so bad." That couldn't be said too often.

"Yeah. Thank you. Soon we'll be able to actually touch, right?"

"Yes. As soon as we can swing it." He didn't intend for another twenty-three days to go by.

"Swing, batter batter."

He stuck out his tongue. "Be good." He knew he needed to let Mason go, but he didn't want to. "Okay, honey. I'll call tomorrow."

"Tomorrow. I'll eat. Bye, Mister."

They hung up, leaving Noah aching a little, so he opened up the browser on his tablet again, determined to search for some dates he could take at least three days off and head up to Colorado.

He needed to see Mason. He needed to touch. Hell. He just needed, and it had been a long fucking time since he hadn't gotten what he needed. Noah had no intention of getting used to the sensation.

Chapter Twelve

"OH my God. Oh my God. Oh my God. Boss! Boss!"

Mason looked up, his head throbbing. "Rach. Seriously. Migraine."

It was so bad his teeth hurt. His hair hurt. His eyeballs hurt.

She looked at him, one eyebrow lifting. "If you're that sick, you should be at home."

"Pardon me?"

"Seriously. Sick people in an office aren't appropriate."

"How do I always end up with the evil assistants? Why can't I hire people that will be good to me?"

"Because this is a cutthroat business and it's your job to be the nice one. Anyway, I think I just booked my biggest job so far." She bounced, her retro-eighties bow flopping against the front of her shirt.

She had a thing for Reagan-era power suiting, despite her tender years.

"Yeah? Good for you. Tell me all, in your best inside voice."

"Team building." She moved to the little sideboard he used as an office storage cabinet and pulled out some pills. One antinausea, two Excedrin. "Thirty people. Food, facilities, events. Games and a big cookout to wrap it up."

"Yeah? Girl! Good job!" He took the pills she offered. "When did they want it? Do we know what type of venue they want and where?"

Thirty people. Probably Denver. Most companies didn't want to shuttle people too far….

"They did. I've already called the venue in question, and they're open." She paused, chewing her lower lip. "They want the second week in August."

"The…." No wonder they ended up hiring them. Every other event planner on earth said no. His head throbbed. "Fuck. Okay. Okay, let's get to work on this."

A tiny part of him felt so pissed. They were dead in August, at least partially, and he'd been planning to go see Noah.

"Yes!" She yanked her fist down in the air. "Okay, so they have thirty people. Some can stay together; some will need their own accommodation. They want at least two plated meals; the rest can be buffet or continental. They'd like that cookout at the end, and they need conference space as well as games and such. I called Mr. Nixel, and the Leanin' N is available then."

"They're okay with driving in from DIA, or do they need transportation?" They needed to work up a proposal, and that would make a difference.

"According to the personal assistant who called me to make the reservations, some guests will be flying into Aspen on a private aircraft, and the rest will take direct flights from Dallas to Grand Junction. They'll need bus service to the ranch from there."

"Oh? Private aircraft?" He made notes, a niggle of… not worry, but excitement, anticipation… tickling him. "And they knew about the ranch?"

"Yes. She said the Leanin' N was their first choice. One of the guests wants Mr. River as a fishing guide."

"This is for the Wright Corporation?"

"How did you know?"

"I know Mr. Wright very well. I just did his sister's wedding in June." *Oh, Noah. You are so getting a Skype call tonight.*

"Oh! That was the one where your former assistant quit?" Rachel began to look a little uncertain. "Are they demanding and awful?"

"No. He hooked up with the groom's brother and ran to Hawaii."

"For real? That's… that's so romantic."

He glared. "Do not get any ideas."

"None. I have a girlfriend. She's a ski instructor. She would kick the ass of anyone who tried to sweep me off to Hawaii." Rachel smiled. "So, what do I do next, boss?"

"We write up a proposal. You get on the phone about shuttles; I'll talk to Ford about the venue and the food."

"You got it. Buzz me if you need me to make any other calls." She clicked out of the office on her high heels, and Mason made a mental note to invite her and her girlfriend to supper.

First, though, he had to call Ford.

Tonight? Noah Wright's ass was his.

Chapter Thirteen

NOAH loved to fly, but for this trip, he'd let Alan, his alternate pilot, do the flying. This was team building after all. He really did do his annual meeting in August, though they generally went to New Mexico or Wyoming. Time to team build, right?

He handed Jonah Hosteen a beer. Jonah was one of his best friends, all the way back to middle school. "Happy to have a week mostly off, man?"

"You know it, bro. I mean, I like most of your board. Daniels is a stuck-up turd. Promise me I get to make him ride a bucking bronco or make him mud wrestle or something?"

"Totally." He winked. They would find something suitably humiliating for all of them to do, no doubt. They always did, and he had Mason on it.

Mason was both amused and scolding about the whole Wright Corp team-building week.

Mostly, though, he thought his lover was pleased. He'd needed to see Mason, and this was killing two birds with one stone. He could have Mason for a week, especially since he was hanging on for a few days after.

"You look tickled as a pig in shit," Jonah murmured. "You must really like this place."

"I really like this guy." Only his closest friends had flown with them on his private jet, so Noah felt fine talking about Mason. Hell, he was excited for some of the guys to meet his lover.

"So he's an event guy? That's cool. What's he like?"

"He's busy." Noah chuckled when Jonah stared. "No, he's really organized and loves his job. He's… he's kind. You know? And has a wicked sense of humor." Jonah didn't need to know about the mind-blowing sex.

"You do like him. Usually it's all about the blow jobs with you."

"Ew!" Gene Frost just shook his head across the aisle. "Y'all wake me up with your noise and I have to hear that?"

Jonah snorted at Gene. "Like you're not all about the blow jobs."

"Yes, but I prefer them from a long-haired blonde with huge boobs."

"Me too!" Jenna Gantry was the last of the three amigos, and she moved from the love seat in the back where she'd been napping to grab a beer. "Are we dishing on Noah's love life?"

Jonah nodded. "We totally are. He's got it going on with the wedding planner."

"Well, if you get serious, you can have him do your wedding," Gene said.

Noah started tossing popcorn at all of them. "Stop it, all of you."

They all laughed together. They'd mocked him when he hired them all, told him he was being stupid, that they were too young, too close.

He'd followed his gut, though, because it was the right thing to do. They'd proven him right and them wrong. They were a hell of a team.

"When is your dad coming up?" Jenna asked.

They'd all laughed at how excited Daddy was to be going fishing.

"He's going to show up halfway through. Momma has a doctor's appointment day after tomorrow that he wants to take her to."

Daddy had not embraced the whole personal driver thing. Not at all.

"Nothing serious, right?"

"Nah." They would have told him if it was. "Sammy and Doug liked the drive, and they wanted to bring Frank, so they're driving."

"Good Lord. That dog." Gene shook his head. "At least he likes being in the car, I guess."

"He does, and he loves Quartz." He got a bunch of blank stares. "The ranch we're staying at. He's the… teen? Tween? Who took care of Frank when he was up. Sammy thought he would love a play date."

"That's cool that there's someone that can deal with dogs. So, this place? I see it's been renovated. Is it as cool as the website says?"

Poor Jenna. She was not into roughing it.

"It's not a five-star hotel, but it's as posh as you want it to be. They have a hot tub, the food is without question some of the best I've had, and the cabins are air-conditioned and they have Wi-Fi." He'd made sure

Jenna's cabin had some extra girly touches, like feather pillows and a spa basket.

"You are good to me." She leaned over and patted his knee.

"I know. You're the one who compromised this year." Jenna had been jonesing for Reno. "Momma will want to shop in Aspen with you."

"Excellent. That's the best type of team building."

"I thought you'd agree." He winked. God, he loved his job, working with his friends and family. Even when it kept him and Mason running in circles trying to find time. Now they had a week, and Noah wanted it to be magical. "Maydell wants to shop too. Y'all treat her right."

"Have I ever been mean to her?"

"No." Gene was rolling. "That's Jonah the Dragon Lady Slayer. The only man on earth that's made her cry."

"Hey, I didn't mean to!"

"Much," Jenna whispered.

"She just feels very out of place with all the executives and such. Momma will help, as they're of an age, but she'll need a little encouragement."

"She's a battle-ax. She'll be fine." Jonah winked, and while the words were mean, the tone was gentle. They all adored Maydell, and Jonah had made her cry once because he'd given her a birthday card with a pair of pearl earrings to replace the ones she'd lost on a trip.

They were family.

"We're descending, folks. Twenty minutes to wheels down," Alan said from the cockpit.

They all buckled up. "I have my own ride to the ranch, y'all." Noah grinned. "You have a shuttle."

"What? You dog!"

"Are you going to meet your fuck buddy?"

"You're deserting us for a blow job?"

The ruckus was gratifying. He did love to make waves, after all. Noah just smiled and sat back in his seat, thinking of all the ruckus he intended to cause with Mason. Excitement rose in his chest. All the phone calls in the world couldn't make up for a real kiss.

"Your cheeks are all red, bud." Jonah nudged him with one elbow. "Glad to see you all happy to see someone. You deserve it."

"He's special, Jon. I mean, genuinely. Weird, huh?"

"God yes. I mean, you're a bazillionaire. You could have a dozen boys every night." Jonah laughed out loud. "But you want this guy in Colorado."

"I do." He more than wanted Mason. He thought he loved Mason.

"Then go for it. You know how to get what you want."

"Thanks, man. It means a lot that you've got my back." Jonah always had, even back in high school when he'd come out to Jonah by trying to take a drunken kiss. And gotten socked in the mouth for his trouble.

It probably wouldn't happen that way now that Jonah had decided he was omnivorous, but these days, Noah knew what he wanted.

They were on the ground in no time, even if Jenna spent the last five minutes of the flight squealing over their angle of descent. Shit, he was glad he'd let Alan do this flight.

Note to self: Aspen airport is intense.

They landed and filed out, grabbing their little carry-ons.

"Our bags are going to meet us at the venue, boss?" Gene asked.

"They are. Alan arranged with the driver to come collect everything. I'll be heading off, but Mason says he could make reservations for you here in Aspen if you want to eat and explore a little before you start up."

"We can figure it out, man. You go and meet your guy and enjoy yourself before you have to be all executive tomorrow." Jonah was a good man.

"Thanks, guys." He waved at them all before jogging toward the airport. Mason was waiting for him down at ticketing.

He saw Mason, his lover in a skintight T-shirt, a pair of jeans that made his mouth water. That had to be for his benefit, and man, Noah appreciated it.

Moving fast, he met Mason halfway, and as tempted as he was to take a kiss, he took a hug instead. "Hey, honey."

"Hey, Mister." Mason's eyes were eating him up. "You look damn good."

"Thank you. So do you. I mean… we're staying at the condo tonight, right?" He'd never make it all the way to the ranch.

"Yes. Dinner's delivered at eight. I need to take you home and unwrap my present."

"Yes." They let go reluctantly, and Mason led the way out to parking.

Now, as soon as they got in the little crossover SUV, Noah leaned over and took a kiss. Hard. Mason was right there with him, hand wrapped around the nape of his neck, holding him close as they devoured each other. Too long. It had been too long, and Noah already knew he wouldn't want to leave.

"I want you. All of you. Over and over." Mason was going to make him lose his ever-loving mind.

"You need to drive, honey. I'm too old to come in my pants sitting in a car."

"I hear you. Let's go home."

Chapter Fourteen

"THIS whole thing with you and Noah is great for my job security, you know."

Mason was going to beat Geoff. "Hush."

"Seriously. I've had to cook for more Texans...."

He snorted. "I totally call bullshit. We all know Colorado would gain twenty thousand feet if the Texans went home."

"Yeah, but these people are rich. Like whoa. And they'll send more people." Geoff winked, up to his arms in pizza dough.

"Yay job security. I need to take that tray of cheese and crackers out."

"My new guy took them."

"New guy?"

"Yes!" Geoff beamed. "I now have an assistant. Tiny. He's amazing. I can't wait for you to meet him."

"Tiny."

"Tiny McGee."

"You hired an elf?"

Geoff hooted. "Right. An elf. Well…."

"Did you want anything else delivered, boss? They asked for a bowl of pickles, so I have to go back anyway. The Cheez-It knockoff recipe is a huge hit."

The deep, deep voice seemed to vibrate the whole room.

Mason blinked. Oh, this was the best thing ever. Tiny the Biker Giant. Tiny the seven-foot-tall, tattooed, beads in his beard, muscle man. "Hey, there. I'm Mason."

"The event guy?" Tiny boomed.

"Yes, sir, the event guy." He held out one hand to shake.

Tiny engulfed it in his. "Pleased. This is a great group."

"It is. I'm glad to meet you." Jesus Christ, Tiny was built-in security.

"The pickles are in the walk-in, Tiny. Make sure there are enough Cokes, okay?"

"You got it, boss."

God, that was cute. When he glanced at Geoff, he got a grin that said everything he was thinking. Lord, Lord.

Tiny trundled out with a big tray of pickles and Cokes, dips and pretzels.

"He's amazing." Mason just had to say it.

"Right? He's like this ball of joy and just as easy as pie. I adore him."

"Queer?"

"As a three-dollar bill."

Mason grinned. "Is there going to be a love match?"

"Oh, honey. I like Tiny. I wouldn't screw him up by having an affair with him."

Mason frowned. Geoff had love-life issues, and he always wanted to snap at Geoff for putting himself down, but how would that help?

"Hey, there you are." Noah peeked into the kitchen. "Can I have a mo?"

Noah could have all his mos. "Of course. Is everything okay?"

"Sure." Noah breathed deep. "Pizza. Oh God. Yay."

"I know, right? That shit is like crack." He smiled, reaching out to stroke Noah's wrist.

Noah grabbed his hand. "I'll give him back here in a bit." Tugging, Noah led him outside.

God, he loved the way Noah smelled, the mixture of spray starch and Old Spice and man. He also loved the way Noah's lips felt on his once they were around the corner of the house and out of sight.

Oh, hello. My love. The words echoed in his mind.

Noah lifted him up on tiptoes and kissed him until his ears rang.

"Better. Why haven't I seen you?" Noah asked.

"I've been working your event, Mister."

"Yeah? Yay. I need your attention now." Noah managed to look both pouty and amused, which was no small feat.

"Do you? Are you needing a private consultation?" *Oh, Mason, you are not being professional.*

"I do. Rachel just came through the gate five minutes ago. Text her and let her know you're in a private meeting?"

"I can do that." He reached out to run one hand up along Noah's belly.

"Mmm. Before we get cooking with oil, baby. If you don't do it now, you never will."

"No one will come looking for you?" There was a tight little nipple right there, waiting for him.

"No. I told the team I was napping. If I actually say that, they avoid me like the plague until I'm ready to reappear."

"Oh, yay." He grabbed his phone. "Text Rach. In a meeting. Do not disturb. Send. Ta-da."

"My perfect lover." Noah dragged him off to the second-biggest cabin. Mr. and Mrs. Wright were in the main one.

"Kiss me?" He couldn't believe he was doing this, slacking work for a hookup.

"Yes." As soon as they got inside, Noah was kissing him over and over. The flame between them just burned hot. It made sense, he supposed, because no amount of skyping and mutual masturbation would replace this. This was real. Not just the sex, but the being together, reinforcing all the things they knew about each other.

"Damn, honey. I want to eat you alive."

"Awkward, but I'm in."

Noah laughed. "That was a euphemism for a blow job."

"I figured that ou...."

Someone banged on the door. "Dude! Ark! I saw you sneak in here. I am not doing a scavenger hunt without you!"

Noah's face went all thundercloud. "I'll be right back." He marched to the door. "Sammy, I'm busy."

"You're canoodling!"

"I am. And you're interrupting!"

"This is not a hookup! You're paying Mason to organize things. You can't just...."

Noah stepped outside, and the noise stopped. He could hear Noah speaking in a low tone, but that was it.

He felt about two inches tall. He knew better than this. You didn't date clients. You couldn't. He snuck out the back door, closed the door quietly, and then he headed back toward the main house, moving as quick and quiet as he could.

When Jonah waved him down, he smiled and walked over, nodding to the rest of Noah's team. He could do this.

"Hey, guys! How are you doing? Everyone comfortable?"

"This is fab." One of the guys, whose name he couldn't remember, had obviously lost the last race or whatever they were doing, because he wore an inflatable palm tree hat, and a pool floatie around his waist said Sink or Swim.

"Can I get anyone anything?"

Sammy slipped into the group, not quite meeting his eyes. Ouch. Someone was pouting.

"Can you send someone with more Sprite?" Jenna asked. He liked Jenna a lot. She had a ready smile and a great flippant humor.

"Absolutely. I'll take care of that right now. If you'll excuse me." *Sprite. Sprite. Sprite.*

He texted Geoff, just so—*oof.* Noah caught him before he fell, hands on his arms. "Where did you go?" Noah kept his voice low but definitely, er, commanding.

"I went back to work. I have no interest in getting you in trouble."

"Mason, I own the company."

"I know, but…." Surely Noah didn't want his family thinking they were… doing exactly what they were doing. "I'm just trying to protect you."

"I love you for that, honey." Noah's expression went wry. "Doesn't mean I'm not frustrated as hell."

"I love you too."

The words sort of crashed down between them, just sploosh, turd in the punch bowl.

I love you too.

Noah's eyes lit up, but then he grimaced when someone called his name. "Tonight. You. Me. I don't care if we have to drive back to Aspen."

"Tonight. Go on. They need Sprite." And he needed to hide his face in the freezer.

"Promise?" Noah stood there, and probably would until he crossed his heart.

"Yes, Mister. I promise."

Chapter Fifteen

EXCEPT it didn't look like they were fixin' to be able to keep that promise that night.

Sammy had started having cramps, and they ran her to the hospital in Aspen.

They admitted her, and Noah and Doug spent the night at the hospital with Mason at the ranch dealing with everything, including his mom and dad.

Mason was a champ, and Rachel was turning out to be a hell of an assistant. Maydell went back to Dallas that night to handle everything down there, and now he had to decide whether to send Doug back to the ranch or get him a hotel room he could run to and wash and such.

How's it going? Mason texted. His lover.

Ok. Tired

I bet. I'm on my way to the hospital to bring you my keys

Thanks so much honey

He would totally stay at Mason's condo.

You need food?

I do. As soon as you come I can duck out if you can eat with me.

Noah thought Sammy was going to be fine. He honestly thought she'd just overexerted herself at high altitude.

k. Doug? Sammy? His man was so generous, so good.

Doug will stay here tonight I bet. He and Sammy had chicken salad and chips.

They looked pretty sad, really, but Doug had wanted to eat with Sam.

cuin20

He looked at Sammy, smiled at her. "This is what you get for interrupting my canoodling."

"Butthead," she teased, but she looked so scared, and Doug was right there with her, holding her hand.

"Be good, Noah. I would hate to kick your butt in the lobby."

"I would hate for you to try to kick my butt at all, Doug. I'd have to wipe the floor with you." He said it automatically, but he wasn't feeling it right now. "I'm gonna have to go eat soon."

"Mason is coming." Sammy smiled for him, brave as hell. "You go with him and go sleep after, okay?"

"I will. I'm going to his place, so we can be here in five minutes."

"Okay. I know you have my back, Ark. It's been a long day. Have something spicy and yummy for me."

"Will do. I will be back in the morning, and someone will bring Momma and Daddy. Doug, I'll get you a room close by."

"If I need it, sure."

"Bubba, you're going to want to take a shower and change, if nothing else." He really just wanted Doug to have a place, even if he didn't use it.

Doug nodded to him, and he could see the deep fear in his eyes.

He clapped Doug on the shoulder. "Do you need me to stay? I can." Noah hated not knowing what to do. He always knew how to handle a situation.

"I think we'll sleep just fine in here and—"

A nurse came to the door. "Excuse me. There's a Mr. O'Reilly here?"

"Thank you. I'll be right out." Noah leaned down and kissed Sammy's cheek. "I'm five minutes away, okay? And I have my phone."

"Love you, Ark."

Noah didn't linger and headed out, finding Mason standing there with a little suitcase, a bag of cookies, a thermos, and phone chargers.

Phone chargers.

Noah was keeping him. Forever.

"Hey." He gave Mason a broad, relieved grin. "Let me take that in for them, and I can go."

"You got it." Mason passed everything over with a smile.

He let their fingers touch, lingering just a moment in Mason's warmth. "Be right back."

"Dude! You rock," Doug said when he appeared with the chargers and cookies. "Now I'm set all night."

"Yep. Okay, y'all are sure you don't need anything else?"

"No. Go. She's sleeping. Shoo."

Sammy had always been able to fall asleep in seconds. It amused him that she'd dropped off the moment he left.

He scooted or shooed or whatever, and met Mason back in the hall.

"What are we eating?"

"We can go to Jimmy's for a burger and a beer or La Creperie Du Village for raclette and a glass of wine."

"What the heck is raclette?" Noah blinked, because he wasn't sure that sounded comfortable. A tiny rack of lamb? A wee kick to the balls?

"Interactive food. Meat and cheese and potatoes. Pickles. Think fondue, but with a grill. It's sort of romantic, you know?"

"Oh." That sounded like heaven. A long, nibbly meal with wine.

"Yeah? I made us a reservation for ten."

"That's perfect. Can we drop by the condo and just let me get cleaned up?" Hospitals smelled. Sure, it was sterile, but he always felt like people could tell, as if they were searching you after they smelled you to see what disease or injury you might have.

"I brought your suitcase, your laptop, and your cords." Mason led him to the parking lot, to the SUV. "I thought you might need them."

"Thank you." He took Mason's hand because the lot was mostly deserted. He didn't want to push, but he needed contact.

"Is she okay? Sammy? I mean, is she going to be okay?"

"I don't know." Noah blew out a breath. "I think they're just keeping her for observation, but she and Doug are terrified."

"Poor baby. I hate that for her. Well, you tell me what you need, and we'll make it happen." Mason headed out of the parking lot.

"You're it, honey. I'm so glad to see you I could just bawl."

"Well, we'll take you home and dress you up and we'll have a nice long meal." Mason reached out for his hand. "Open up the window, feel how the heat dropped."

He took Mason's hand with his, then opened the window with his other. Oh, that was nice. Cool as a cucumber. He liked the way the temperature dropped when the sun went down here. In Texas it could linger all night.

He leaned back and closed his eyes and let Mason take care of him a little bit.

Forty-five minutes later they were sitting at supper, the wine a dry white that would cut through the cheese. A tabletop grill was set up, and it held these little melting trays underneath for the cheese. He couldn't wait to try it.

Mason had him rolling with laughter, genuinely tickled at the tales of weddings and parties. Of the night his goddaughter was born. "I swear to God, I'm standing there, Veronica is squeezing my hand so hard I thought I was going to die, and the guys are down getting coffee!"

"Oh, no! How could they leave you like that?"

"It was supposed to be, like, another three hours, so I said I'd let them have a break. In two contractions, the world changed. I was the one that cut the cord!"

"Did they freak out?" He poured more wine, knowing he was supposed to let the second waiter do that, but he wanted another sip.

"It worked out. They have a birthday planner every year, after all."

"They totally do." Noah shook his head and was about to recount a story of his own, when the cheeses and meats arrived, along with sliced potatoes, onions, and cornichons. "How fun is this?"

"I thought you'd like it. Fun and tasty and weirdly sexy."

"Definitely. Finger foods and tucked away at a table for two where I can feed you with my fingers if I want? Yeah." Sexy for sure. The place had a real rustic, French Alps kind of charm.

"I know it's not a perfect circumstance, but… I'm glad to be here with you."

"I am. Too. With you." He laughed, the wine making him giddy. "So show me how we melt."

"Put some meat and veg on the grill, then pick your cheese and put it in the melter."

They both chose the mild raclette cheese to start since it shared its name with the process, and the melt was on.

Mason played with him, keeping him chuckling, keeping everything sexy and light, charming him and plying him with cheese and wine.

The cornichons cut right through all the richness, and they shared a dark chocolate mousse. He would have thought he'd be stuffed at the end, but all the food was small, and it was lovely and perfect.

"Oh, man, that was good. I even stopped checking my phone for catastrophes."

"Now I get to drive you home." Mason dared a quick kiss, and Noah heated. "I promised you tonight."

"You did. I intend to collect. Why do all of our hot dates have to be at the end of exhausting days?" Someday they would just have a night where they sat on the couch and watched a movie and ate pizza.

"I was wondering that myself, Mister. Seriously, we should just take a vacation someday."

"That sounds perfect. Where have you always wanted to go?"

"Like pipe-dream go or actual-dream vacation?"

"Either. I'm all about making dreams come true." Noah wanted to do something amazing for Mason, who had done so many things for him.

"I'd love to go to Venice one day, but really? I'm saving for an Alaskan cruise. One of the fancy ones."

"Yeah? You ever been on a boat?" He had a yacht docked at the Gulf. They could sail away for a week or two.

"I've been white-water rafting a lot."

"But never on a cruise?" Noah had taken a gay cruise once. Oh God, that would be a hoot with Mason. They would have a ball being able to make out on the promenade.

"Not yet. We should go sometime!" Mason bounced a little in the booth. "When you have time, of course."

"It's probably easier for me to get time than you, honey. I have a huge, well-oiled machine. As long as I can check in occasionally, they can do without me."

"I see how tired you get, Mister. I see you."

"Do you?" Noah stroked the back of Mason's hand. He did get tired because he was the support system for so many people…. He loved them all, but he did get worn-out.

"Yes." Mason nodded, then paid the check, shocking the hell out of him.

He blinked, opened his mouth, and then closed it. Just did it, not a look or a wiggle or a word that meant he was trying to impress.

Damn, this one was a keeper.

"You ready to go home with me, Mister? We have a promise to fulfill."

"I am." They left the restaurant, and it felt almost chilly to his heat-tough Texas skin.

He felt dazed, like he was on the cusp of something he didn't understand. This happened to him sometimes while he waited for his head to catch up with his gut.

Whatever it was, he had a feeling that with Mason along for the ride, it was going to be amazing.

Chapter Sixteen

MASON had his headphones on at seven in the morning, dealing with phone calls from the ranch, where Rachel had set up camp.

"Rach. Rach, you're rocking it. I'm sending a car to pick up the Wrights, and I have a lovely four-bedroom vacation home near the hospital rented for the week. It's empty and on the market, but Nan says they can have it. You need to make sure that the tech stuff is set up so Noah has the choice of coming back to the ranch or staying here, you got it?"

"I'm on it, boss. Is she going to be okay? Mrs. Preston?"

"So far, so good." He stopped and sipped his coffee. "I'm proud of you, girl. Seriously. You rock."

"Thanks. This has all been so crazy." She sighed. "Also, you have a phone conference at two this afternoon. Should I reschedule?"

"I'll take it. I can do it from here or the office or the hospital or the ranch."

"Yep. It's Calleigh from Amazing Cakes. She wants to run her designs and flavors by you."

"For...." Suddenly his mind went blank.

"The Findlay birthday. She's seventy-five."

"Right. Right. I'm on it. Text me fifteen before to remind me?"

"You got it. Laters!" She hung up, and he paused one more time to breathe in mountain air and drink more caffeinated bean water.

He wanted to make this as easy on Noah as he could, and since organizing things was what he did, that was what he focused on.

Noah poked his head out the patio door. "How cold is it?"

"It's not. It's gorgeous." He loved his wee baby balcony that looked out on the mountains. "You get you a cup of coffee?"

"Not yet. Let me get that robe you got me." Noah disappeared, and he laughed out loud. Such a Texan.

He had stuff for toast if Noah was starving, or they could stop on the way to the hospital for danishes and coffee.

Noah joined him moments later, wearing a robe and carrying coffee. "This view makes a man believe in God. I see why so many Texans come here every chance they get. That way we have the best of both worlds."

"It's perfect. In the winter, I get to watch the skiers."

"And in the summer, you get ravens and magpies." Noah was fascinated by the birds.

"Yes. You tell me when you're ready for business, huh?"

"Ugh." Noah grimaced but then smiled. "I slept great. So anytime."

"I've spoken to Maydell. All is well back home. I've arranged a vacation home for your folks and Doug for the week. It is on the market, but it's fully stocked. It'll be available at noon. I do have a car bringing your folks up, and I have Rach setting up the electronics for you to skype in for your meeting this morning."

"You're inhuman." Noah grabbed his hand, toying with his fingers. "How are you this morning?"

"I'm good." Waking up next to Noah was perfect. He was going to miss it desperately.

"Okay. Well, how about we have breakfast. I saw you had bread and eggs and milk. Do you have butter and syrup?"

"I do…."

Noah cooked? Food?

"Excellent. Momma taught me that a man ought to know how to cook one breakfast, one supper, and one dessert. I can make french toast, hamburgers, and peach cobbler." Noah rose and stretched, his robe opening up to show his ripped, fuzzy belly.

"My magical man." He leaned forward and nuzzled said belly. "Sounds delicious. How can I help?"

"Find said butter and syrup and show me where I can find a griddle or a flat pan." Noah stroked his hair. "Breakfast with my lover. Wow."

"I know, right? Don't tell anyone and maybe we'll even get to share another cup of coffee."

"Shh." Noah led him inside, and the next forty-five minutes were… unreal.

Noah cooked perfect french toast. Mason warmed the syrup. They ate and read the newspaper on their tablets and did shit like a real couple.

He was stunned at how easy it all was.

Was it stupid to worry about whether he could keep it? It being this. Them. Noah and his amazing care, the way he loved.

Noah caught him staring while loading the dishwasher and came to him immediately. "Are you okay?"

"Yes. I was fantasizing, that's all. Ignore me."

"Not possible. What were you daydreaming about? Venice?" Noah yodeled out some fake gondolier song that started with "O Sole Mio" and ended with cacciatore.

He started laughing, and they ended up dancing around his kitchen, hooting and hollering like hooligans. Noah was a magic man for sure, but God help him, he couldn't dance. They staggered out into the living room, where Noah tripped over his robe tie and landed hard on the couch, howling with laughter.

He landed on top, his headset going one way, his phone going the other.

Noah kissed him then, a warm slide of lips and tongue that stalled the laughter in his chest and made him moan. The fairy tale might end sometime soon, but right now he had a good thing going, so he had to just go with it.

"Do we have time?" he asked, the words muffled in their kiss.

"I'll make time."

"I do love that about you." The word was getting easier to say all the time.

"I love you too, honey. I really do."

Please, he prayed. *Let that be enough.*

Just let that get them through.

Chapter Seventeen

SAMMY and Doug were on their way home. Everything was stable, and Sammy had marching orders from the doc to see her own ob-gyn as soon as she got home.

The only one who seemed sad to leave was Frank, who had spent a week in doggy heaven with Quartz.

"So what's the plan for today?" Noah asked, poking Mason with his bare toes. They were getting good at this breakfast and newspaper thing. Today they'd done it in bed with cereal and coffee.

"I was thinking we could play naked mayonnaise Twister and then go get tattoos."

"Wow. That's pretty adventurous." He waggled his brows. "But that must mean you don't have a gig."

"I do not. I cleared my schedule."

"Me too. I have at least two more days." Noah sipped his coffee, pondering. They could do anything, everything. He had to admit, there was a peace in staying right here.

Mason grinned at him. "Are we napping and watching movies?"

"Is it bad that's appealing?"

"We could go to the Isis tonight. There's a bar downstairs. It's like this charming little movie theater right here."

"Sounds great." He could totally spend the day just hanging out. Mason made him laugh, made him happy deep down.

"So what would you normally be doing on a Sunday?"

"Depends on the family. I skip church, much to Momma's chagrin, but I'll meet them for lunch." He worked a lot from home on Sundays.

"That's dear. I don't have much family left, and what I have, well, they didn't have a whole lot to do with me. Of course, I'm usually working on Sundays. Someone always has something that was winding up."

"I'm sorry." Noah paused. "I'm out to my whole family, though it's not something Momma and Daddy talk about. Of course, kicking me out of the fold would be a shitty business move."

Mason grinned at him, tickled as a pig in shit. "Yeah, I can see where that would be awkward. Sammy seems to be okay with it. Me, less so."

"You're not okay with me being gay?" He threw up his hands in mock horror.

Mason snorted in his coffee cup, damn near choking himself. "You bitch."

"I am." Noah sobered. "I'm sorry your family gave you a hard time."

"Eh, I have another life, another family now. I have what I need."

"I hope I'm part of that."

"You don't have to fish. You know how I feel about you."

Noah snorted. "Still new enough to need reassurance."

"You got what I need." Mason rolled over, snuggling them together and kissing him on the cheek. "All the way, Mister."

"Good deal." He kissed the corner of Mason's mouth. "Where's your remote?"

"Uh… somewhere…. We were watching last night."

Noah dug it out from under Mason's butt and copped a feel while he was at it. "Have you ever been to Dallas?"

"Not yet. I just recently got an invitation to visit, though."

"I know! You should come down. See my place." He wanted Mason to sleep in his bed, ride down and see the ponds on his land, swim in his pool.

He wanted Mason to share his world. He'd never felt that way about anything. The TV was loud as hell, so he turned it down. "When can you come?"

"If I make a few phone calls, I can fly back with you."

"No shit? Oh, honey, that would be perfect." He gave up on the TV and glomped onto Mason.

"Mmm. Hello." Mason grabbed him, kissed him hard. "Do I know you, Mister?"

"Better every day. Mmm." He'd never done this in his life, lounged in bed with a man he loved. There was not even a niggle of work guilt.

All those tight little muscles and they were all for him. No wonder he was basking. He stroked Mason's belly.

"Can you make those calls today?" Noah asked.

"I'll see what's on my schedule, but I'm fairly sure I can, why?"

"Because we can fly down in the morning. I have my plane, after all."

Mason blinked. "Right. I've never known someone with their own plane. I've probably worked with people, but... that's incredibly fucking cool."

He knew. It was. It blew his mind. Still. Sammy never thought anything about it, but he could remember wearing Goodwill clothes and having his momma cut his hair. Now he had his own motherfucking airplane.

Noah kissed Mason's neck just below the ear. "Cool. I'll file a flight plan."

"Okay. I'll make some phone calls and clear the next... how many days?"

"How about three, at least. Maybe four."

"I can do that. I'll free the week, and that way I have a little leeway."

"Thank you." He took another soft kiss. "That means a lot to me."

"You're welcome. You want to walk down and find brunch somewhere after we do a little business?"

"Sounds like a plan." He would have to make some calls as well, but he would move heaven and earth to make this happen. It was time to bring Mason into his life as well as the other way around.

He rolled to the edge of the bed to grab his phone off the nightstand. He would start with the airport. Hell, he had no idea whether Alan was still in town or if he'd flown the others back down to Dallas the day before.

If Alan had, the son of a bitch could just fly right back.

He was bringing Colorado to Texas.

Chapter Eighteen

MASON felt like he'd been kicked in the teeth a little bit.

This was the biggest place he'd ever been in, barring the Stanley, which was a hotel that looked like a mansion.

Noah wasn't wealthy. He was rich.

Like "here's my limo, here's my plane" rich.

Like "I have a staff" rich.

Like whoa rich.

He had to admit, he'd expected something grand and exciting, but this was intimidating. "Dude, I think your master suite is bigger than my condo."

Part of him had to wonder if Noah had been embarrassed by his little place with its not-so-custom finishes and tiny footprint.

"I think it is, honey. You have the view, though." Noah shrugged out of his dress shirt, showing off that tough body.

"I do." He put his suitcase at the end of the bed, then headed over to look out the window and found a lovely section of the wraparound porch.

"There's a little door over by the dresser if you want to go look." Noah nodded toward a different section of wall.

"Yeah? Cool." He went out, the heat hitting him like a wall. Jesus. Humid. Hot. God.

The porch was amazing, though, the sunshades keeping it from being unbearable, and there was a little suite of patio furniture with cushions that invited him to enjoy the view of the pastures. Everything was greenish brown right now, with the late August heat, but it was still pretty.

"Let me turn the ceiling fans on. That'll cool it off."

"Your porch has fans?" He glanced up. Huh. Look at that.

"It will be really nice out there tonight, for sure." Noah joined him on the porch, looking almost redneckish in his T-shirt and jeans, a cap in his hand. "I hate to rush around, but Lee wants me to come down and look at some issues with the second pond. Want to come with? I'll take the four-wheeler."

"Sure. Let's go. Let me put some jeans on." He was dying in this heat, and he'd worn shorts. He grabbed some Levi's and pulled them on, then put his shoes back on. "Ready."

"You're a champ." Noah handed him a cap. "I know you do sun, but the heat can just be wicked here." Noah dropped a kiss on his mouth before steering him out to the side yard, where a garage building held three four-wheelers, a lawn mower, and two Bobcat machines.

Soon they were off and running, flying across the pasture with Noah talking to him a mile a minute. He didn't hear but every fourth word, but that was okay.

The gist was that Noah loved it here.

He hung on tight, and they finally pulled to a stop next to a pickup truck, which yielded an older man with bowed legs and tanned-leather skin. He wore a cowboy hat and Wranglers, his boots so old they had a hole at the toe.

"Lee, this is Mason. Mason, Lee. What's up, man? You been breaking things on me while I was gone?"

"Well, not me. Your cousin Jeremy."

"Oh, for fuck's sake. I told y'all not to let him touch anything."

"I hear you, boss. What's wrong is the drain feed from the upper pasture is all cut off. I got no idea what he did, but one of our good auger bits is stuck in there."

"Goddamn it! How do we fix it?"

Lee spit on the ground. "That was why I called you down. We're gonna have to hire it done, or we'll end up with a real mess first time it rains. I tried to get it out, but that drain is old, and I'm afraid it'll collapse."

"Let's do it, then. I'll take every dollar from Jeremy's hide. Little shit."

"Sorry, Noah. I was tryin' to keep an eye on him."

"Have you checked all the machinery? If he lost an auger, he might have burned out an engine."

Mason stared, stunned at this version of Noah. His lover knew how to work the land, clearly, and understood heavy machinery. Which, okay, oil. That had to be a thing.

He stayed quiet because he had nothing to offer. He wasn't even totally sure he knew what an auger was.

His phone vibrated, and he grabbed it. Rick.

Having fun

Yeah.

You answered really fast to be having fun

There's a problem with an auger and rain

A WHAT

Fuck if I know. Something to do with water

Oh. We aren't big on that here. Is it hot?

There wasn't an inch of him that wasn't sweating.

OMG OMFG

I figured. Flew through there once where I had to get off on the tarmac. Jeezus

I'll bring Jaycee a cowboy hat

Bring us something too!

Greedy!

He would have to ask Noah what sort of quintessentially Texas thing to take to his friends.

Miss u. Come visit soon. And call me!

Promise.

"You ready for the grand tour, Mason?"

He slipped his phone in his pocket. "I am. Did you decide what to do?"

"Lee will call Ray Tyler for an estimate. He's a good guy. Come on, huh? I'll show you the whole kit and kaboodle."

He nodded and followed along, and then they were off again, zooming over little rises. There were cattle and horses, donkeys and barns. It was stunning, completely different from what he was used to but gorgeous nonetheless.

They visited Sam's place, and he got to love on Frank before they zoomed back to Noah's home. They stepped inside, only to be met by a sweet-faced lady with tall hair. "Mr. Noah. Are you dining in tonight? Maria has time to cook if necessary."

"Hey, Barb. I think we will, yes. I'm thinking enchiladas, if there's time."

"There is." Barb smiled at Mason.

"Oh! Mason, this is Barb. Barb, this is Mason. He's here for the week."

Mason held his hand out to shake and gave her his best smile. "Pleased to meet you."

"I'm pleased as punch, sir. If there's anything I can get you, please let me know."

"That's normally my line."

Barb blinked and gave him a slight smile.

"He's an event organizer, Barb. He's always running."

"Oh? Oh, you did Miss Sammy's wedding. We saw the photos. Beautiful job. Are you arranging something here?"

He looked to Noah, not sure what he was supposed to say.

"No, hon, he's just visiting with me." Noah said it easily, but something in his voice told Mason the answer was very calculated.

"Of course. If you need anything, y'all know where to find me."

"Yes, ma'am." Noah took his hand once Barb was out of the room, tugging him toward the bedrooms again. "I bet a shower would be good, huh?"

"I would be all over that. I'm sure I stink."

Noah had said he was out to his parents, but Sammy had been stressing anyone knowing about them sleeping together. He wondered if maybe Noah was a little less out than he liked to pretend. Of course, maybe Mason was just feeling out of place himself and filtering everything through that.

Oh, look at him, being all psychobabble man. Lord, he needed a cold drink and a bath.

"Want a Coke? I have a cooler out on the porch." Noah led the way through to that amazing porch, where sure enough, a vintage Coke cooler sat tucked against a wall Mason hadn't really seen.

"That rocks. Do I need a dollar?"

"Nope. I have the key." Noah winked. "I make Jeremy pay for them."

He leaned forward. "Can I kiss you?"

Noah raised that one brow he was so good at. "Of course you can, honey. Come here."

"I'm a little sweaty." Still, he came, didn't he? Yes, he did. He wanted that kiss more than he wanted his next breath.

Noah slid a hand behind his head, tugging him close and pressing that hot mouth to his. Noah tasted like the mints he popped constantly when he was in the air. Mason thought Noah had learned to be a pilot because he hated to fly and wanted to be in control.

Mason got it, he guessed. He liked organizing events because that was like juggling, and that was vaguely the same thing.

Noah kissed him hard on the mouth, proving he wanted closeness, contact. It felt so fine, Noah's body pressed against his, hand like an iron bar against his back.

Moaning, Mason tried to scale Noah like Mount Sneffels, his body already on fire.

"You're hungry…."

"Is that bad?"

Noah's phone began to ring, and he sighed. "That's Sammy. Let me answer it."

Mason nodded and backed away. Sammy might need something about the baby. Of course she had to come first.

"Hey, baby girl, whatcha need? Yeah, yeah, that was us. Mason flew down with me. He moved his schedule around."

Mason wandered, wondering if he should unpack his bag or if he was going to end up in the guest room.

"No, Maria is making enchiladas. I can tell Barb to send some over. No, I want to have supper with just Mason."

He found the en suite, smiling at the huge, fancy-assed bathroom with a whirlpool tub and a walk-in shower. The tile was immaculate and looked maybe a year old, from the style. He wondered if that was because Noah redid his place every few years, or if this master was a recent add-on.

He wanted that Coke, so he headed back out, more than willing to put his dollar in if Noah was still on the phone.

"Hey." Noah smiled, shaking his head. "Here's the key. Bet you thought I forgot, huh?"

"I thought you may still be on the phone, more like."

"Sammy wanted to come up for supper. I told her no." Noah led the way back outside. "I adore her, but she has to have some boundaries."

"And she needs to rest, hmm?"

Noah got them each a Coke. "She does. But more than that, she needs to back off."

Mason frowned, sinking down into one of the patio chairs. Maybe they needed to talk about stuff. Noah seemed so agitated about Sammy. "From what, exactly?"

"Oh, you know. She's bored. She's pregnant. She's wanting to be a part of everything right now. You get it? I don't have time for babysitting in my life."

"No. I guess not." Mason turned the Coke between his hands. "Maybe now was not the best time for me to come down."

"Nonsense. Nonsense, don't be like this, honey. I just want to pamper you a few days. What do you think of the ranch?"

"It's beautiful." And that wasn't a lie.

"Thanks." Noah sat next to him, reaching for his hand. "I like having you here."

"It's not weird for you?"

Noah looked right into his eyes. "It's going to take some getting used to. I've never brought anyone home before. I imagine I'll screw up."

"Not ever, huh?" He got up, then moved to sit in Noah's lap, no matter how hot it was. "I like being your first, Mister."

"I like it too. I really do. Don't give up on me yet, okay?" Noah nuzzled his cheek, then licked his lower lip.

"I don't intend to." He let their lips meet, let the kiss go deep for a long minute before he backed off and took another drink of his cold Coke.

It was damned hot, and who knew what would happen before he got his shower?

Things were just a little crazy around here.

Chapter Nineteen

NOAH hummed, rolling over to touch Mason's back. He frowned when he found nothing but sheets. Damn. He thought they'd had an exceptional night. He'd even turned off his phone around nine just to get some time alone.

He heard tip-tapping coming from the porch, then a soft little chuckle. "Who do you belong to?"

Noah grinned. Talk about up with the sun. Mason liked his porch and patio time in the mornings. He rolled out of bed, then pulled on some pants so he could step outside.

There was a little purse dog—something fluffy and bouncy—up on his side porch. "What the hell?"

"Not your secret love puppy, I take it?" Mason teased.

"Not one bit." He stared. "She's a tasty bite for coyotes."

"No way. This is not New Mexico. No coyotes." Mason reached down over the railing to pick her up, almost going ass over teakettle.

"Oh, we got 'em. That and feral dogs. Big pigs. Basselopes."

"If you try to sell me on snipe hunts, I will beat you down, Mister."

"I bet Stoney River told you about those." In fact, he'd bet that's why Mason sounded so self-righteous.

"I bet you'd be right."

"You can take the boy out of Texas." He bent to take his good-morning kiss, and damned if that wee dog didn't growl at him. "Oh, I don't think so, you little shit."

"Hey, now." Mason was barely holding in that sparkling laughter. "She's a princess."

"A princess? Does Ms. Priss have a collar?"

"No, but she's been taken take of, you can tell. Someone will be missing her. Don't you have, like, dog wrangling staff? Even the Leanin' N has dog wrangling staff."

He was going to beat Mason's butt.

"Lee keeps a few border collies for work, and then there's Frank, and Daddy's pit, Lily. Not much to wrangle. They all wear collars, though."

"You want some water, Miss Priss?" Mason went to take the dog into the house, and Noah shook his head.

"No, you don't. No stray dog fleas in my bedroom. Let me call someone to take her into the mud room."

"She doesn't have fleas!" Mason was tickled as a dog with two tails.

Butthead.

"How do you know?" Noah ducked inside to grab his phone. "Barb? Hi. We got a stray dog. We need flea wash until we can figure out where she goes. No, Mason will bring her. Oh, and some water and a cookie."

The silly thing's ears went up when he said cookie.

"Also? Coffee and food. Coffee first."

He nodded at Mason's little laptop. "I'll put that in, and we can go around on the porch."

"Thank you. Is it okay, just having the robe on?"

"No one is shy. Daddy wanders around when he comes up for the pool in this… well. It's very Italian." Noah rolled his eyes. "And awful. Come on."

Mason started giggling like a loon. "Are we going to use the pool today? Do you have an Italian pool boy?"

"No. Brazilian."

"Oh, wow. Is he pretty?"

"She's stunning. She has a great set of fake boobs, or so I'm told."

"Dude. Seriously? You have the opportunity to make the great queer cabana boy fantasy come true and you blow it?" Mason stopped. "Hey, Miss Barb."

"Hi. Oh! Oh, no. Poor baby!" Barb looked truly stricken. "That's Miz Perry's dog. She passed on last week, and that no-account daughter of hers said she would take her."

"That's awful! Does anyone know her name at all?"

Lord have mercy, Mason's here for less than a day and this happened?

"Priscilla."

"See!" Mason crowed. "Priss."

"Barb. Clean. Disinfect. Feed. Coffee?"

"Coffee is on the table. I'll get Lee to come up and take care of it. Is it staying here until we find it a home?"

Noah glanced at Mason, who nodded hard. "Yeah. Have him bring up a crate for night too."

"Softy," Barb whispered, and Mason cracked up again.

"Mason likes her, I reckon." Noah grabbed a cup and added cream for Mason. "What's Maria making for breakfast?"

"Migas. Does that work?"

"Are they as good as Noah's french toast?"

"Mmm. No. But they're better than Sammy's biscuits and gravy."

"Sammy has time to improve," Noah said.

"That little girl has you wrapped around her finger," Mason teased. "It's so adorable."

"Yeah, yeah. I know."

"Spoiled is what she is." Barb snorted. "I'll go call Lee."

A middle-aged Hispanic lady bustled into the kitchen. "Hola, Mr. Noah. Migas?"

"Yes, please."

Mason took his coffee, drank deep. "Oh, that's good."

"Mr. Noah is a snob," Maria said.

Noah tugged her apron string. "And you're mouthy, lady."

"You know it." She winked at Mason, then started bebopping around.

Mason spoke softly. "I think you just fixed it right."

"Thanks, honey."

"How do you like your eggs, Mr. Mason?" Maria asked.

"Over medium."

"Good, good." She hummed while she worked, and soon enough they had migas.

Noah actually loved her migas. Spicy and creamy, with strips of fried tortilla…. Yum.

Mason ate with him, not saying much, drinking his coffee.

He wasn't sure if Mason was uncomfortable or worried about work or what. Noah hoped like hell his life wasn't turning Mason right off.

"You okay, honey?" Because he had to.

"I am." Mason looked at him and whispered, "I'm just trying not to make you uncomfortable with all your people."

"Oh." Damn. "Well, could you talk to me anyway? No one is going to bite."

"Nobody but this damned beast." Lee strolled in with Miss Priss, the growling little mutt wrapped in a towel. "Someone else want to take this? I think it's a vampire."

"I'll take her. She seems to like me." Mason took her, and she settled right in.

"Crazy."

"Want a plate, Lee?" Maria asked.

Lee winked at Noah. "Only if it's paper. I need to head back down to the barn, so I can't stay."

Good man. He knew what was what.

"I'll watch the dog. I know you guys are busy." Mason smiled a little shyly.

"Thanks, buddy. I appreciate it." Lee took a Chinet plate full of migas and ran.

"Coward!" Noah called.

Lee flipped him off, and he was thankful Mason didn't see it. Not that Lee didn't do that once or twice a week. At least.

Mason chuckled. "So, what are our plans for today?"

"Hmm. Is there anything you want to see?"

"I need to get some touristy things for my girl and her dads, but other than that, I'm open."

"Well, then, we should spend some quality time in the pool, huh?"

Mason lit up like a Christmas tree. "That sounds amazing. I love to swim."

Bingo. "Then come into my parlor."

"Your very wet parlor?" Mason teased.

"Yep. We have swimsuits. Let's go get changed." Noah rose and kissed Maria on the cheek before leading Mason out of the room. They would get changed and swim and splash and maybe have a cookout tonight.

He sure hoped that silly little dog could swim.

Chapter Twenty

MASON sat at the huge outdoor kitchen and dining area that was apparently shared between the Wrights. Sammy and Doug were there along with Mr. and Mrs. Wright and about ten thousand different family members who either wanted to ask Noah for something, meet Mason, or get free food.

It was loud and boisterous, everyone running about and playing football in the heat. The beer was running free and loose, and there were kids everywhere.

Crazy.

Even when he had been talking to his family, any get-togethers they'd had were low-key. Playing cards and watching movies, maybe.

Noah was flipping burgers, laughing at something his dad had said, and he was so pretty he made it hard to breathe.

Frank and Prissy were playing. Well, Prissy was playing. Frank was collapsed on his side, letting her jump over him again and again and again.

It was a good thing Frank was a good-natured beast. Priss wasn't, but Mason was so damned in love with her already. Lee had brought up a crate, and from somewhere, Barb had provided a bed for it. Leopard print with pink trim.

This was so odd. Usually he was in the back of a party, running things, keeping things organized. Not watching it from the front lines.

Everyone was very kind. They wanted to know all about Colorado, so he had no lack of things to talk about.

He noticed that with all the kindness, he was never once even face-to-face with Noah, never close enough with his lover to talk. Noah had waded toward him more than once, but it had never happened. It was as if he'd been culled from a herd.

At some point, Mr. Wright and a couple of other men drew Noah away toward one of the barns, and he was about to follow when Mrs. Wright plopped down beside him with a sigh.

"Are you enjoying our little cookout?"

"I am. This is an amazing setup."

"Noah and his daddy planned it all out. They went to the Lowe's and had one of those meetings, you know? Boys and their toys."

He smiled, but his toys involved project management software and snowboards. Still, he nodded and smiled, because he was a master at small talk.

She grinned over at him, and he could see where Noah got his eyes. "How long are you staying?"

"I'll have to get back to Aspen in a few days. My business needs me. I've been handling it from here, but

I have events that require personal attention." And the mountains were calling.

"Ah." Something in her tone made him look at her more closely. Her smile never faded, but she said, "That's probably good."

"Is it?" Ah, the worried mother speech. At some point, you were too old for that, right?

"Well, this is Texas, sweetie. We all know Noah prefers men, but he does have a lot of people depending on him. He's a busy man." She just kept smiling, like a crocodile. "You see, it'll be better for both of you to keep yourself up in the mountains. They're more liberal up there, and you can be proud and all, run your little business, and Noah can have an outlet. I mean, he's an oilman. He has a certain reputation."

He stared at her for a second, the white noise in his brain threatening to make him say something unkind. "I would never hurt Noah, Mrs. Wright. I care for him."

"Of course you do, that's obvious."

"And I'm not interested in interfering in his business dealings."

She blinked at him like he'd lost his mind. "Well, of course not. It's not like you'll be marrying in or anything."

Don't do it. Don't say anything. Mothers are just that way.

"Please don't be offended, Mr. O'Reilly. I wouldn't want you to feel like…."

"Part of the family? No, ma'am. I don't think that will be an issue. If you'll excuse me, I need to get Miss Priss fed." He stood and scooped up his pup and headed back through the dark toward Noah's house.

On the way, he called Rick. "Hey, can you please arrange me a one-way ticket to DIA? I need a seat for me and one for my dog. First class."

"For when, babe?" Rick didn't ask the why, which made him grateful.

"Tomorrow. Not too early, but not late. I want to come home. I'll rent a car to get home."

"Bullshit. It's beautiful in Aspen right now. Jeff and I will drive you. A dog?"

"I found her. She's beautiful. Miss Priss."

"Are you okay?"

"Sure I am. I got the matriarchal 'don't hurt the reputation.' I've heard it before."

"Did she at least write you a check?"

"No, go figure. However, I am allowed to keep seeing him so long as I do it in Aspen and promise not to marry him."

"Ouch. Oh, babe, we love you." Rick sighed. "So, first class, you and Miss Priss. What kind of pup is she?"

"Shih Tzu and Papillon mix?"

"Oh, good Lord."

"Yes. She will bite you so hard and smile doing it. I adopted her today." He would get her a rhinestone collar and a leash with those rainbow sparkles.

Rachel would adore her.

"We can't wait. Love you. We'll see you tomorrow with bells on."

"Thanks, Rick. I mean it." He hung up so he could hunt a bowl and some food for his girl. Barb had to have procured some food when she got the bed.

"Mason? Are you in here?" Noah's voice came from by the back door, and this was as close to his lover as he'd been since Sammy dropped by for lunch.

"I am. I was looking for puppy food for my girl." He kept it light, because it wasn't Noah's fault that he needed to go home.

"Oh, I think Barb said she put some cans in the pantry." Noah came in and went to the sink to wash his hands before moving to Mason's side. "Burgers are pretty well done."

"That is an amazing setup, man. You Wrights can throw one hell of a party."

"Thanks." Noah watched him carefully. "You're upset. What happened?"

"Just the standard 'you're not good enough for my son' talk. Nothing special." There was no reason to lie. Noah wasn't stupid, and Mason wasn't upset so much as disappointed.

"My mom?" Noah sighed. "I'm sorry, honey. I really am. She can be so protective."

"I hear that's common. Don't worry, I have her permission to see you so long as I stay in Colorado and don't marry you."

Noah's face went kind of slack with shock. "Oh, wow. Well, it's a good thing I'm not the marrying kind, huh?"

Funny that no one ever asked him if he was. "It's okay, Noah. I'm going to head home tomorrow, I think. I have work waiting for me. Rachel is starting to panic, and I know your people are stressing too."

"Wait, what?" Noah took his wrist in a light grip. "I thought we had some time."

"Mister, I get more face time with you when I'm in Aspen, and we both know it. I can't just sit here when there's work back home."

Noah stared at him for a long moment, his face grim. "I don't want you to go so soon, Mason. Please."

"Tell me you have time to spend." He knew better, but Noah was breaking his heart.

"I cleared my schedule." Which was a nonanswer. So much of what Noah did every day was unscheduled.

Everyone wanted a piece of him. Mason understood. He really did. But he was bored and hanging around. He felt useless with the ranch stuff, and he was… lonely.

"I know. I did too. But—"

Noah's phone rang, the ringtone like an air-raid siren. "Shit. That's an emergency. I have to take it. I'm sorry."

"No worries, Mister." He was doing the right thing. He really was. Noah had a life. He had a life. Hopefully their lives would meet every now and again.

He dug out food for Miss Priss, then watched her eat while Noah stepped out of the kitchen with his phone. If he wanted commitment, well…. He was getting a dog, wasn't he?

Chapter Twenty-One

"NO. No, I don't think that's going to work for me. You write up a new proposal, and I'll look at it Monday." He thought Mike Levain was a good man, but he was asking for a lot of money for improvements to a shared drilling operation, and ecologically it would just be better to shut the thing down. More cost-effective too. "I need something that's going to make it worth the work and make it less damaging to the site, Mike."

He hated turning people down, but that seemed like all he was doing lately.

Noah checked his cell phone since he was on his office phone with Mike. He'd texted Mason earlier, and he was hoping for a reply.

It had broken his heart to see Mason go, but he got it. He did. Hell, he hadn't even been able to tell Mason goodbye in person. He'd had to leave for a site that evening. Mason had been decent, but Noah thought his lover was hurt, angry.

So much for pampering Mason and getting him to fall in love with the ranch. He would be lucky if Mason ever came back.

He hadn't been able to face his momma either, not knowing she'd warned Mason off. That was pushing too damned far.

No reply. Damn. Mason had a small convention he was running through Saturday, but Noah had hoped.

His phone beeped, and he grabbed it, sighing when Jonah's name popped up.

Dinner?

Not the best company today

Stop pouting and come bend my ear. I'll buy

Where

Pick u up in 10

Shit, was he still on with Mike? "Sorry, Mike, did I space on you?"

"I'll get you what you need, Monday."

"Thanks, man. Sorry, I was just out of it for a minute. I appreciate it." He would work something else for Mike too. A counter. He wouldn't leave the guy without income.

"Yeah. Talk to you."

He hung up his office phone, and then his phone beeped again.

He checked it, relieved as hell when Mason's name popped up.

Hey u. Miss u like crazy

Miss you. What are you up to?

About to serve supper 2 40 buttheads. U?

About to go to dinner with 1. Jon

Ah. U home 2morrow?

I am—he would be come hell or high water—*Skype? Please. Gotta go. Love!*

Noah found himself beaming when he walked out of his office. Mason always made his day better. "Maydell, why are you still here?"

"Noah, dear. I was wrapping up those reports for the EPA. I thought you'd be off already."

"I'm heading out to dinner with Jonah. Can you call Bill and let him know I won't need him?"

"Of course, dear. How's Mr. O'Reilly?"

"Good. Doing a convention this week."

"Tell him I said hello, would you?" She smiled at him, just as decent as could be. She liked Mason. Too bad his mom hadn't taken the same time to get to know his lover.

That probably wasn't fair. Momma was a momma, and she was a bear. Maybe he'd go talk to her after all.

"I will. Let me walk you out to your car."

"Oh, thank you, dear." She chattered at him on the way out, and he hated to admit he missed most of it.

His mind was on other things. Personal things.

"Noah, can I give you a bit of advice?"

"Of course." He never said no to anyone older than him when they offered.

"At some point, you have to let yourself have what you need most, no matter what. I won't be indelicate, but Mason loves you. Any idiot can see that."

"I know. I love him too." He did. So much it hurt every day they were apart. Like an open wound.

"Then do something about it, dear. I know my boss. He is not an idiot."

"No? Sometimes I wonder." He bent to kiss her cheek. "Thank you."

"You're welcome. Tell Jonah to be polite."

"I will. Not that it will do any good." Jonah would take him to someplace fancy and burp the alphabet or take him all the way out to someplace like Billy Bob's or Southern Junction and get in a bar fight.

It might be fun, believe it or not. Noah could totally blow off steam and call in sick tomorrow. That way he would be there whenever Mason wanted to skype.

He needed to see his lover, face-to-face.

Chapter Twenty-Two

"**BOSS,** you have the numbers for the ski week proposal?"

"Right here, Rach. I'm at the ranch, for fu…."

"Family harvest festival, boss. Language."

"Right. Sorry. I've got the printouts. As soon as Stoney's done with his hayride, we'll meet. Thanks for the reminder."

"No worries. I'll talk to you then."

He clicked off his phone and took a deep, deep breath. Okay. Mason just needed to go kick off the three-legged race and he could sit a minute.

The families were amazing—mostly gay couples with a handful of lesbians and some poly families having a weekend of costumes and spooky stories and hayrides.

Stoney was having a ball.

Ford kinda looked… bemused every time Mason saw him. He thought Ford was rather like his Noah. He'd been used to a very different life before returning to the Leanin' N.

Now Ford was holding a little girl and assuring her that monsters weren't real and that he would find her daddies straightaway.

"Can I help?" Mason smiled gently. "What are your daddies' names, sweetie?" Ford had dealt with one kid. Quartz. This was more Mason's area.

"Daddy and Da."

"Well, let's find them." Really, all he needed to do was search for two panicked fathers and he could be a her—

There they were.

"Look who's here!"

"Daddy! Da!" The little girl squealed. "You finded them."

Ford handed over the wee one with a strained smile, and the two dads piled on effusive thanks.

"How do people do that?" Ford asked. "Have those little creatures, knowing they'll give you heart attacks?"

"Ask your husband, man." Although he wouldn't be opposed to a baby. Jaycee was the light of his life.

"Nah, that was stupid luck. Ask him to tell you that story one day." Ford winked. "Apple cider?"

"Yes, please. This seems to be a good event, huh? Everyone seems to be having a good time."

"It does. I like it. It's low-rent but high-entertainment for the dollar. I think we ought to do it again next year."

"You know where to find me. Stoney is having a ball." The cowboy was dressed up like an Old West stagecoach driver, complete with huge drooping mustache.

"I know. It's unnatural." Ford dipped up hot mulled cider. "It's great to see Angie wrangling that team."

"And Quartz is doing great with the pony rides." Stoney and Angie rescued ponies from terrible conditions and fostered them at the ranch. Rather than making them walk in circles, Quartz led each pony out with a rider one at a time, leading them around the paddock. "You've made a cowboy of him."

Ford snorted. "That boy's going to be the most illustrious engineer in history."

"Yeah?" Now he knew what to get Quartz for Christmas. Some kind of building set. He owed the kid for dog wrangling.

"Yep." Ford peered at him. "We hoped we might see Noah this weekend."

"I haven't even talked to him in a week. He's very busy." Obviously. Because they hadn't skyped in three of those weeks.

"Oh." Ford flushed. "Sorry, I just assumed. Sorry."

"It's okay. He's…. He's married to the corporation. I'm his consort, so to speak."

"That sounds sad, Mason." Ford held up his hands. "I mean, your business is your business. I'm sorry if I'm out of line."

"We're friends, aren't we?" He had Rick and Jefferson. Rach. He wanted to count the Leanin' N group among those friends.

"We are. I might even have a unique perspective on Noah's side of the situation. Maybe he needs help understanding that just because you've done something one way a long while doesn't mean you can't change it."

"I don't want him to change, Ford." Mason shook his head, sighing softly. "I love him. I love that he's driven. I just… I don't know. His life is so huge and full and electric, and mine is… not."

He had Miss Priss and his condo and work.

"Don't sell yourself short. He told me how much he admired you after the wedding. How you handled everything with a cool head and a warm heart."

"We're not breaking up. I'm just… lonely." Maybe he should see if Noah could come up for a day or two around Christmas. They could go on a sleigh ride and drink hot cocoa….

"Call him." Ford winked.

"You two look too serious." Geoff joined them, peering into the cider container. "Refill. How are the cheese pumpkins and crackers holding up?"

"Tiny is doing a glorious job, Geoff." The big man could make a cheese tray.

"He's amazing. Okay, I've got cupcakes cooling to be frosted, and the kids will all take back a goodie bag. Am I missing anything?"

"I don't think so. We're almost done. It's been a good day."

"It has." Geoff didn't bother with polite hands-off advice like Ford. He just gave one of the best hugs ever.

Mason took it. He needed it. Hell, he needed it bad.

Geoff held on until it was time to let go, he guessed, and Mason thought he might just make it through the day.

His nights? Well, they belonged to Miss Priss.

A SOFT knock on the door of his home office had Noah exploding up out of his chair, cell phone in hand. Really? He was just about to finally sit down to call Mason and someone was fucking knocking?

"What?" He flung open the door, ready to tear someone's head off.

"Don't you fucking snarl at me, Ark. I am fat and grumpy, and I will kill your ass!"

Noah sighed. "I love you, Sammy, but you have the worst timing."

"Like that's news. Can I sit?"

"Come sit with me in the front room. The recliner is way more comfy than my meeting chair."

"It's fine." She brushed past him into his office, so Noah closed the door.

He sat behind his desk, steepling his fingers on the wood top.

"So, why aren't you still seeing the party planner? Was it Momma?"

"What? I was just about to call him when you showed up."

"Jonah says you love him."

"I do."

"So why is he in Colorado? Is he too good for us?"

"No. He thinks we're too good for him." He raised a hand when she opened her mouth. "That's not entirely fair."

"Ah, it was Momma."

"Yeah." Dammit. And damn Momma too for putting this wedge in between them. "Hell, Sammy, what if that's not all of it? What if he came down and saw my life and decided not to buy into the Wright insanity?"

"Why on earth would he do that? You got everything a person could want." Sammy rubbed her belly. "Is he still with you?"

"I think so?" He sat back, rolling his head on his neck. "It's been three weeks since we could skype. I mean, he's answering my texts, he's calling. I miss him so bad, but it's like the universe is conspiring to keep us apart."

"If he loves you, he'd make the world move to get y'all together."

Noah blinked. Okay. Okay, sure, but why was that Mason's responsibility alone? "How do I make time, Sammy? How do I get all of the calls and emergencies and meetings to stop long enough to go?"

She stared his ass down. "When they call you, you tell them to call me. Or Doug. Or even Daddy. Jonah knows all your damn passwords. If I call you? Then you panic, because your nephew is coming. Otherwise, you don't answer your damn phone. Ark, why do you think I went traveling for so long?"

"Because you're a free spirit who likes to break the rules." He didn't even think hard on that.

"And because I needed to just do something that wasn't about being a Wright. Just for a little while."

That left him blinking again. "Is it so bad?"

"Hell no! I appreciate every single thing you've given all of us. You and Daddy both, but it comes with pressure." She stroked her belly again. "It means a lot of people depend on you. But you have the right to find someone who makes you happy and rearrange things to be with him." She shrugged. "The man isn't going to steal you away from us. That's not possible. But maybe… shit, maybe you can focus on something just yours."

"I want to try." He did. "How do you and Doug do it?"

"First, I told Doug's daddy to suck it up, I was marrying him. Then I took him away for a while and proved that he was more important than anything else."

"I can do that." He could. He would figure this out. More than anything, he knew he needed to do whatever he was going to do with Mason face-to-face.

"I know you can. I do. I love you, Ark. I'm sorry if I messed up anything for you."

"No way. If it wasn't for you, I would never have met him. Well, that and he thought you were two grooms."

"Yeah. I blame Trev."

That was the new saying around the Wright Corporation. People who weren't even at the wedding were heaping blame on Mason's former assistant.

Trev and Bryan were engaged and talking about moving someplace more friendly. Not Colorado.

"I love you, Sammy. You want some chips and salsa?"

"Oh my God. You have pickle slices to put on top?"

"That's nasty, Sammy."

"Uh-huh."

"I have pickles." He stood, reaching out to help her out of her chair. "Thanks, baby girl."

"I love you, Ark. I want you to be happy." She groaned and stretched. "Heavy baby."

"Soon, grasshopper."

She shot him a glare. "You don't get to tell me."

How many times had she said that to him since she learned to talk?

"Come on. I need your help plotting."

"You make chips and salsa, I'll plot."

With Sammy on his side, he could hardly lose. Two Wrights couldn't make a wrong. Or whatever. Time to implement plan "Get Mason Back."

Between Sammy, Maydell, Rachel, and him, Mason was doomed.

Chapter Twenty-Three

"BOSS?"

"Yeah, Rach?" Mason was heading for the coffee shop. He was craving a hazelnut latte. It was November, snowing, and he needed a shot of sweet, sweet caffeine.

"Are you going to shoot me in the face if I book you next week?" Her voice was a lot excited and a little nervous. "A client is coming into town for personal reasons and wants to talk to you about setting up a wedding next year. Says it will take two or three meetings."

"Did I have anything else set up next week?" Lord, he had a headache.

"Nothing I couldn't reschedule."

"Is this a big contract?" He wasn't sure if he wanted the answer to be yes or no.

"Potentially an engagement party, a shower, and a wedding, apparently. Complete with rehearsal dinner."

Oh. Oh, he couldn't turn that down. Not only that, it would be an easy week. "Rock on. Do it. I like meetings. Book a conference room, and I'll get a few pastries and coffees. Speaking of, want a latte?"

"Oh God yes. Peppermint mocha, please."

He fully expected to show up to the office soon and find Rachel wearing reindeer horns. She loved her holiday stuff. It actually made him happy, believe it or not. She reminded him why he'd chosen this business.

"Peppermint mocha it is. I'll be there in a few."

"Okay, boss. Oh, cranberry orange scone?"

"If they have one, it's yours."

He ordered, getting a scone for Rach and a bagel with cream cheese for him, then pulled to the side to wait and then grabbed his phone.

Miss u. Hope ur day is good

The reply came with gratifying speed: *Not bad at all Yay! Mtg w/new client next week. Crosses fingers*

Good luck honey

Thnx. Love you.

He did, even though he was beginning to believe that Noah had moved on a little. He'd hoped they could get together for the holidays, at least for a few days, but he worked weekends, and Noah worked weekdays.

Love you. XXOO

He laughed softly and pocketed his phone. Silly Texan. Mason thought he was the most wonderful butthead on earth.

Which was why he still held out hope of surprising Noah with a Christmas meet-up. Just a few days between Christmas and New Year's.

If Noah couldn't come to the mountains, then he would go to Noah.

Chapter Twenty-Four

NOAH hosted Sunday dinner at his place. Maria had made tamales and chili, and everyone wanted to come anyway, but this time Noah had an agenda. This was a prayer meeting with his family and best friends, because he was going to change the rules, and they all needed to know up front and have a chance to figure shit out.

Everyone piled in, Barb taking coats and gloves. Sammy was the size of a house, waddling over to the stuffed chair that he had put there, just for her. It sat higher than the rest of his furniture, so she could get up easily.

Noah waited until everyone was set and looking at him curiously. Yeah, with Jenna, Jonah, and Gene there, the family unit had to be wondering what the heck was going on.

"Hey, y'all. Thanks for coming over. I know everyone is busy this time of year." He grinned. Making them do this before feeding them ensured attention.

"Is this a meeting to plan the Christmas party?" Gene asked. "Because it's blackmail to hold up tamales."

He chuckled. "Nope. We can talk about that over lunch. I wanted to talk to all y'all about something else." The only one not there was Lee, his head wrangler. He'd told Lee his plans and gotten a long, measuring look. Then Lee had nodded and spit on the ground.

"I run all this shit, anyway," Lee had said. "No big deal."

Noah did love the cowboy way.

Sammy smiled at him, nodded. She and Doug knew his plans, and so did Jonah, and he had their support, so that made it easier.

Nerves curled in his belly like a big snake, ready to strike down his confidence, so Noah just launched right into it. "So. I've been doing a lot of thinking, y'all, and I've decided that I need to step back a bit." He held up a hand to forestall his momma, who had already opened her mouth to protest. "I'm not quitting my job or moving out of town permanently or telling anyone to take a flying leap. What I am doing is rearranging my life to get a little more time for myself and to do what makes me happy."

He pulled out a pile of stapled papers. "Maydell will be emailing this information to you after this meeting, but here is a list of the people in charge of different situations. When I am out of pocket, the only phone calls I will be answering are Sammy's and Jonah's."

"What?" That was a chorus, and he shook his head.

"I promise I'll open the floor in a minute. Jonah is stepping up to do a good bit of the business stuff, but,

Gene, I'll depend on you for the foreign markets, and, Jenna, I'll need you to coordinate more of the financials and communicate with Sammy about the charity arm."

This had been way easier in his head. Jonah was nodding, but his folks and Jeremy and his Uncle Tom looked unconvinced.

"I need to be able to live my life, y'all. I love this company, but it's not enough."

"Rar!" Sammy said. "It's about damned time!"

"Samantha!" Momma stared at Sammy, aghast.

"What? It is. We all get to be part of something more than the family and the company, but Noah doesn't because he's gay? So not fair."

Jonah's eyes went comically wide. "Noah's gay? Oh my God!"

"You are not funny, young man," Momma snapped. "Of course we want him to be happy."

"Then help me do this. Maydell has agreed to train a couple more people on her systems, because she would like some time off as well. We've set up a timeline for that, but diversifying is good."

"As long as she hires them," Jenna said. "She'll know who can read minds and wear their superwoman costume under their business suits."

Maydell laughed out loud. "Miss Jenna, you are a treasure."

Jenna blew her a kiss.

"You children are not giving this the seriousness it deserves!" Oh, Momma was pissed.

"Oh, Momma, do give it up. He's a fudgepacker. Your tolerance seams are showing. Noah loves Mason. Mason loves him. Let it go." Sammy was getting less and less ladylike as her belly swelled, and she hadn't been particularly ladylike to begin with.

"Oh dear God." Daddy rolled his eyes. "Are you moving to Colorado?"

"Not full-time, no. I will be there part of the time." He hoped. If Mason turned him down, he sure was gonna look like an ass.

He was going to go into this like Mason cared for him as much as he loved Mason.

"Well, y'all can stay in that house by the hospital. I liked it, so I bought it."

Noah blinked a little. "It's a nice house." He had no idea what he would do about Mason's condo, but that was Mason's decision, not his. He wasn't going to demand anything. Only offer himself.

"Anyway, Lee has agreed to handle the properties. He and I will meet once a week either in person or online." Lee skyping. The idea made him cackle. "Emergencies will go through Doug, as I think he really has a handle on maintenance."

"I do. Y'all know I've been working hard to be useful."

"You're always useful, baby." Sammy was smitten. No question.

Noah got it. He really did. Not to mention that Doug was into land stewardship and eco-friendly ranch techniques, which Noah loved.

"Okay. I know y'all will have questions, but that's the gist of it. I'm heading up to Colorado tomorrow for at least a week."

"Are you sure about this, son?" Momma asked. "Are you really sure?"

He smiled at her, meeting her gaze without flinching. "I am. I really want to give this a try, making a life with someone. Mason's it."

She sighed, then nodded. "I'll cut his balls off myself if he hurts you, baby boy."

"Woo!" Sammy punched the air. "Go, evil Momma."

Noah rolled his eyes. "We're all good?"

Even Jeremy nodded, wide-eyed but clearly willing to go along with everyone else.

"It'll be rough at first, but we'll figure it out. Hell, it's the holidays." Gene grinned over. "It's not like any of us intend to work for weeks."

"Ass." Noah felt as if a huge weight had lifted off him. "Thanks, y'all. It means a lot to me, your support."

"You're family. That's what we do," Daddy said.

"It is." He couldn't stop grinning.

The whole meeting had gone better than he'd expected.

Now he just had to hope his talk with Mason went as well.

Chapter Twenty-Five

MASON made his way across town with a box of doughnuts and a huge thermos, his crate of contacts and his laptop. Lord, this snow.

He parked as close to the door as he could, then pulled his wheelie crate out and stacked everything up.

He hummed a little, making it a game to avoid the icy patches on the sidewalk. The conference rooms were at an office building, so the salt stuff was out in force, melting away the snow.

He waved at Kathy at the concierge desk, then went to grab someone from the events office to open the conference room for him.

Lord, it was a nice space, but beige? Oh my God.

He set up the food and coffee, then put some classical music on his computer and started spreading out pictures and flyers—venues, cake, flowers, candles, invitations.

There was a lot of rainbow in there. Rachel assured him she had checked. Two grooms.

He chuckled and sat to wait, taking a second to grab his phone and text Noah.

Happy day Noah. Miss u.

The sound of a text tone playing the wedding march made him spin around, his mouth dropping open when he saw Noah standing in the doorway behind him.

"Mister?" He stood up and ran over, grabbed Noah and pulled that gorgeous son of a bitch down for a kiss, damn his clients.

Noah kissed him back, all but lifting him off his feet, that big body swathed in too much fabric. It didn't matter. What mattered was that Noah was here, and it was the best surprise, the most wonderful gift.

Noah finally let him slide back down to the floor so they could catch their breath. "Hey, honey. I'm not interrupting am I?"

"I have a client. I'll call Rach, have her come down." Rachel could handle it. She'd have to. "This is the best present ever."

"Uh." Noah smiled gently. "I'm your client."

"What?" He searched Noah's eyes. "Really?"

He was going to kill Rach. And give her a bonus.

"I swore Rachel to secrecy. I know how hard it is for you to rearrange your schedule, and she promised me you had one event this week and she could do it with her eyes closed." Noah beamed, looking so tickled with himself.

"You're amazing. Seriously. I have doughnuts. Coffee." They wouldn't need the rest.

"Do you?" Noah took his hand and led him to the table, then plopped down in the big chair at the head of the table before pulling Mason down on his lap. "I do love doughnuts. Are there maple?"

"I always get two of those." A silly sentimentality, but it made him happy. "And there's good coffee."

First, though, kisses. He brought their mouths together again, letting himself sink into them. He wasn't going to miss this opportunity. Noah was here, and it was an early Christmas miracle.

He'd been so damned sad, worrying that they were going to drift away from each other and that was that, but these kisses meant that, even though they weren't going to see each other much, when they did, it was perfect.

Noah held him tight, finally just resting a cheek on the top of his head. "I missed you."

"Yes. I was worried. It's been so long." Months.

"I know." Noah sighed, breath stirring his hair. "I have so much to talk to you about, and some of it scares me half to death." When he stiffened, Noah stroked his back. "No, it's not bad. I swear."

"We're not breaking up?" Because as teenaged-angst as it was, it was true. It was the last thing he wanted.

"No! I mean, please tell me that's not what you want." Noah tilted back to stare at him.

"I love you, Mister. You know that. I want you." Simple as that.

"That is the world's most perfect answer." Noah kissed him again, then again for good measure. "I might need a doughnut for moral support."

"Moral support? Okay, hold on." He brought the box over, along with the thermos and two cups. "Ta-da!"

"You're amazing." Noah grabbed one maple pastry and munched. "Mmm. I was light on the food this morning."

"Did you fly up this morning in this weather?"

"Alan flew me into Grand Junction early-early, and I drove up." Noah had a chocolate cream next. "Yum."

"And now I get you for a whole week?" There was so much they could do, starting with a few shared orgasms at the condo.

"I hope for way more." Noah chuckled, wiping his hands. "This is gonna sound super businessman of me, and this is so not business, but it's the only way I know."

"All I need is for you to be you, Mister. What's up? Seriously." He wasn't sure what Noah was up to, but the nerves were obvious, and that was wigging him out.

"I want us to try to be together. I mean together-together. My phone? In the glove compartment in the car. I mean, I'm still going to be busier than a one-legged butt kicker, but I've worked hard the last month or so to rearrange everything." Noah's green eyes held uncertainty, but also so much hope.

"I don't understand. What are you talking about, exactly?" Because he wasn't going to be Noah's boy toy. He liked working, most of the time.

"I'm talking about us making a life together, Mason. Splitting our time between here and Dallas. We can do it and not have either one of us have to give up what we love to do."

"How?" How on earth would that work for them? "Come home with me? I want to talk, but… there's something else I want more."

Noah nodded, rising to hold out a hand to him. "Bring the doughnuts. We'll need our strength."

"I need my things. Give me two minutes." He gathered all his papers, putting them back willy-nilly. He could organize them later.

"I really do have a wedding to plan. Well, to pitch to you, anyway."

"Really? You want to use the Leanin' N? I checked this time, two grooms. Oh! Oh, Trev and Bryan. How funny!"

"Right? Bryan's dad said he wasn't interested in even attending, so I thought I'd throw them a wedding." Noah held the door for him before taking his laptop bag.

"That's sweet, Mister." He could do something easy and fun. "Did you know when?"

At least he knew what Trev liked.

"Trev wants an Aspen wedding, so I would say just after ski season when it's cheaper for people to come up." Noah helped load his gear. "I'm in the Escalade over there. I'll follow you."

"Good deal. You can park in my spot, and I'll park in visitors'. Be careful."

The snow was still coming down, big white flakes that were going to make the guys up at the slopes happy.

"I'm much more confident this time." Noah winked at him, and they separated reluctantly.

The drive to his condo seemed endless, and all these worries started popping up. How was he going to split his time? This couldn't work. It couldn't. This was a pipe dream that Noah had thought up. Together? Noah was a Texas oil baron billionaire, and he was a wedding planner in a one-bedroom condo, and that didn't blend.

Noah seemed to have a plan, right? He should listen at least. Give Noah that.

Hell, if nothing else, they had this time, right? He wasn't going to look a gift Texan in the mouth.

Noah was right behind him, and they met at the stairs up to his condo, Noah having slid smoothly into his parking spot. "Hey."

"Hey you. You take the food, and I'll get this." It was a long three stories up in the cold.

"Got it." Noah tucked the thermos under his arm to grab the doughnuts. He led the way up, and Mason noted the cowboy boots had been replaced by hikers.

Logical. Those boots were slick as snot. Even Stoney River switched to lace-ups in the wintertime.

They got inside, set down all the stuff, and for a long moment, they simply stared at each other. Noah's lips looked a little blue.

"You want the fire or the bed, Mister? You look cold as ice."

"I want you." They met in the middle of his living room before heading to the bedroom, and Mason was grateful Miss Priss was hanging out with Rach at the office today.

"Come to bed, Mister. I'll warm you up." He held one hand out, wanting his lover in his bed.

Noah took his hand, following, and they stripped down before sliding between the sheets, laughing when cold hands met warmer skin.

"Damn, it's frigid out there," Noah said. "I need longies."

"I'll have Rach grab you some." Later. Much later. Right now he wanted more.

He wanted kisses and touching and something that didn't happen by his own hand while Noah was so far away.

Noah kissed him, leaning on one elbow next to him, lips warming quickly. He scooted closer, bringing their bodies together, shoulder to hip.

They rubbed a little, finding all the ways their bodies fit together. Rediscovering each other.

"I never wanted anyone like you, honey." Noah rolled atop him, covering him totally. "My little hard body."

"No?" He knew it was true. He felt the same way. "I was missing you so badly it's like I conjured you."

"Maybe you did. Maybe you called to me."

Maybe he had. Mason wanted to believe. He leaned over and nipped Noah's shoulder, knowing the sting would surprise his lover to no end.

"Toothy!" Noah laughed for him, one leg pushing between them. "Gonna mark me as yours?"

"No. No, I know I can't. I was playing with you." He leaned back, looked at the spot that wasn't even pink. "See? All safe. I have your back, Mister."

"I don't care, honey. I'm all yours. Now, if you left it right under my ear, I might protest a hickey…." Noah was chortling, eyes dancing.

"Poor abused man." He chuckled softly and wrapped one leg around Noah's hip.

"I am. I abuse myself so often it's criminal." Noah drew one of Mason's hands down and wrapped his fingers around Noah's shaft. "Touch me."

"As long as I can." Pillow talk, sure, but he meant it, every word. Mason stroked up and down, pausing when Noah returned the favor, fingers finding his cock, exploring the tip, then the flared ridge of the head.

He forced himself to keep his hand moving, keep the rhythm up, even as Noah tried to drive him out of his mind. The slow caresses made him dizzy as a bad fall on the slopes.

This was way more fun than that.

Noah licked Mason's lower lip, then nibbled a little. Sharing the wealth, he guessed. He lifted his chin. He had nothing to hide and plenty of turtlenecks.

Damned if Noah didn't latch right on above his collarbone and pull up a mark. Lord, the man could suck, which gave him ideas.

He left himself wide-open, offering every inch.

Noah hummed, a cross between an approving sound and a chuckle. Then he moved down to lick at one of Mason's nipples, exploring. Mason's body tightened, his balls drawing up as Noah sucked, tongue sliding over the tight bud of his nip.

He shuddered. Noah made him so hard. So hot.

Those surprisingly hot lips slid down over his belly, Noah's beard stubble scratching his hip.

He tried to sit up, and Noah shook his head. "Let me love on you. Please, honey."

"Anything," he whispered. "Anything at all."

"I want to taste. It's been too damn long." Noah's words buzzed against the head of his dick, the vibrations almost too much to bear.

"Months."

"Never again."

He nodded, but honestly, Noah was sucking, and he would have agreed to anything—anything at all—to make Noah continue.

Noah didn't tease any more. Lips sealed around Mason's shaft, he bobbed up and down, tongue working at sensitive spots in both directions.

Every so often he'd open his eyes, stare and know that it was his Noah, not some great wet dream. This was his lover, and the pleasure Noah gave him built and built until Noah pushed one finger between his asscheeks, tapping at his hole.

"Love!" He bore down, took that finger in deep, and shot, as eager as any untried teenager. It had been too long.

"Mmm." Noah took him in, every drop, then slid up his body to kiss his mouth. The kiss was flavored with him, and he whimpered, then reached out and wrapped his fingers around Noah's heavy prick again.

That was what Noah needed, that big body bucking wildly, Noah riding his touch.

He groaned, pumping hard, palm rolling around the tip with every upstroke.

It took maybe a minute before Noah was taking his mouth with a fierce kiss, hips jerking as Noah came for him. Hot and wet, Noah's seed fell on Mason's skin, marking him far better than any hickey.

"God, honey. I needed that bad."

He understood that.

Shit, he more than understood that. "You warmer now?"

"I'm on fire, honey." Noah held him close, heart thundering against his ribs, every beat obvious to Mason.

He wrapped them together in his goose-down comforter. "I'm so glad you're here, Noah."

"I am too. I needed to see you. I know I could have called, but this was too important." Noah rested their foreheads together.

"Sometimes you need to breathe the same air."

"Yes. And I needed to look in your eyes and remember you care as much as I hope you do." Noah smiled, lips curving against his. "I do love you. That's the most important part. Remember that when I get all imperious."

"Imperious, huh? Wow."

"Right? One disadvantage of running everything is expecting everyone to be on board right away with my every scheme."

"Do you have a lot of schemes, Mister?"

"With you I just have one." Noah met his gaze head-on. "Find a way for us to be together most of the time. I know we'll both have to travel. I know we both need to work. That's the kind of people we are. I just don't see why we can't make the effort to do it together."

"You're way more important than I am, Mister. I know that. I'm the guy people like you hire."

"Hey." Noah took his chin in one hand. "How can you say that? If we're going to do this, we have to come at it as equals. Your time is just as important as mine."

"Yours is a lot more expensive." They had to acknowledge that. "And I have to say, a lot of people need you."

"Yeah. I'm working on that." Noah paused, the laugh soft and kinda self-mocking. "I have spreadsheets to show you."

"Spreadsheets? I love spreadsheets." There was something comforting about having that much information in a searchable form.

"I adore you. Seriously."

Mason kinda felt as if he was on top of the world. Noah had really put effort into this.

He just needed to figure out what *this* was.

Chapter Twenty-Six

ON the second day they were together, they made love all day. In between naps. By day three, Miss Priss had stopped trying to bite him, and Noah thought that was some kind of victory.

By day four, though, Noah was starting to worry. Mason was loving, happy and smiling, but studiously avoiding anything like a discussion about the future.

Then the night of day four, Mason started murmuring things about how the week was flying by so fast. As if Noah was really going to just go back to Texas in a few days.

Noah set the alarm on his phone for the next morning so he'd be up about a half hour before Mason got up to have his coffee and newspaper.

He set up his paperwork, his agreements, along with a folder holding his final volley. He opened the door to a super quiet knock, Rachel standing there with lattes and croissants.

"Thank you," he whispered.

"Anytime. If I'm going to be your assistant here, as well as the boss's, we're going to have to hire someone to help with the event planning."

"We totally will. Can you take Miss Priss?" He liked Rachel. He really did. And he thought she'd make a great Aspen-based assistant for them, if Mason approved.

"I can." She flashed him a beaming smile and tiptoed inside to grab Miss Priss up right in her crate, since the little lady was sleeping. "Holler if you need anything else."

"You're amazing, lady. Thank you ever so."

He closed the door, hearing Mason wake, snuffling and snorting.

So cute. He usually didn't get to hear that. He took the croissants to the kitchen and laid them out on a pretty plate before setting them on the tiny dining table. The chocolate ones looked decadent, but there were plain and bacon-and-egg as well.

"Mmm. Do I smell coffee, Mister? You're up early, love."

"I know. Latte?" He looked Mason over carefully. Very carefully, because the brief shorts did little to cover that hard body.

"Did you go out?" Mason stretched up, flat belly rippling, shorts sliding down to show those golden curls.

His mouth went dry, and Noah almost let himself be distracted. His eyes wide, he watched that spot, but he forced himself to answer. "I asked Rach last night. She brought stuff over and took Miss Priss."

"Aw. That's cool. Good morning." Mason came to him, all slinky kitty as he begged for a kiss.

"Morning, honey." Noah gave that kiss happily, hoping for just this the rest of his life. "How are you?"

"Happy."

Simple as that. Happy.

Thank you, God.

Noah hugged Mason tight. "Me too. I figure we have a nice leisurely coffee and croissant, and then you owe me a meeting."

"A meeting? You want to plan Trev's wedding? Now?"

"No. I want to show you my spreadsheets, talk about how we're going to split our time and such." He held his breath, hoping Mason didn't blow him off.

"Let me start the fire. That'll make it nice in here."

"Sounds good." He got out two more plates, some butter, and a little carafe of orange juice.

Mason tugged on his heavy robe and then settled, grabbing a pad and a pen. "I'm ready, Mister. Let's work this shit out."

"Okay." He nodded and gathered his stuff. "Okay." He was as nervous as he'd been giving his first presentation to Daddy's investors. "The spreadsheet here"—he called it up on his laptop—"basically tells you who I've turned what over to. After this week, I've set aside an hour on most mornings to take calls from everyone, but my only emergency calls now will come from Sammy or Jonah."

Mason blinked, looking over the information. "You mean… is this for vacation?"

"No. This is permanent. If I'm on vacation, only Sammy will get an answer unless there's a prearranged emergency call. I finally got my family to understand I needed to limit access some. I'll have changes to the schedule when it's time for board meetings or site visits, of course, but basically I've delegated a lot to carve out personal time. We deserve it."

Mason stared. "You're serious. How? I mean, you're serious? You want—you're really serious."

"I am." Noah's heart thundered, and he knew if he took a bite of croissant right now he would barf.

"Okay. Okay, I need to process. Let's talk this out. What about my company? I have… I mean, I'll be honest, I have a mortgage and a car payment. It would be hard to make my bills on an hour a day for me…."

Noah nodded. That wasn't a no. Mason didn't quite understand yet, but even so, it *still* wasn't a no.

"I'll have to work more than an hour a day, honey. That hour I set aside is for phone calls. Not including the occasional conference call. Mainly that's just so my family know they can't expect me to be available twenty-four seven." He reached out for Mason's hand. "I would never expect you to give up your business. Or your condo, come to that, though I would love for us to look for someplace a little bigger with the same view. That's a goodly bit up to you, though. I love your condo." Noah gathered his thoughts a moment. "The only change I can think with your business is we might see how it works for us to share Rachel. She could train someone else to do some of the party work, and she could sort of work for both you and me as more of a personal assistant."

"I love my condo too. We could… the offices next to mine are empty. We could work together here, if you have a place for me in Texas? I can't ask you to give up your ranch. I wouldn't."

"My family understands that we're together. I want you to be with me, but if you want to live in Dallas and go to the ranch for special occasions, we can figure it out." That was the easy part. He knew it was all rich bitch of him, but he could afford to live anywhere. "If you need an office in Texas to work out of, the Wright building has offices we rent. I bet I could make you a good deal."

Mason gave him a look. "You think?"

"I do."

"I want to organize all the Wright functions."

"Oh?" Noah felt like shouting with joy. "Are you trying to negotiate with me, O'Reilly?"

"You bet your sweet ass I am, Mr. Wright."

"You do drive a hard bargain. Okay, so we roll living situations into next quarter's business. I stay here with you and Miss Priss for now, and rent the offices next to yours for my Colorado headquarters." Noah rubbed his thumb over Mason's hand. "If the fam comes to visit, Dad has bought that house you rented for us. They can stay there."

"And I want to spend Christmas with you—no matter where we spend it. In fact, I want New Year's too."

"Man, I give you an inch…."

"I want all of you, Mister. If we do this, we do it right."

"We have to go down to Texas a week before Christmas to do the annual Christmas party. I'll get you with Maydell so you can review her plans. But then I thought…." Noah pulled his trump card and slid the envelope over to Mason. The best part was he hadn't needed it. This was just gravy now. He knew Mason was in with him. For life. "Christmas."

The first-class flights left Dallas December 23 and returned from Venice January 3.

Mason looked at them, then looked again, his lips parting in obvious shock. "Noah. Noah, these are for…. Oh my God. You're serious?"

The little table damn near went ass over teakettle when Mason pounced him, kissing him hard enough that it would surely bruise.

Noah laughed out loud, holding Mason close. "Merry Christmas, Mason. Want to go to Venice?"

"Yes. Yes, Rachel's going to kill me, but yes. To all of it." Mason held him, fingers framing his face. "This isn't about the money, though. You know that, right? I would love you if you had nothing."

"And I would love you if you didn't have the best view in Aspen." He kissed Mason again, because he could. "Trevor has offered to help Rach over the Christmas hump. To make up for running off. That means you can enjoy without worrying. Much."

"Is this real, Mister? Are we going to be together?"

"I'm sick of missing you. Of living for everyone else. I want us to be real. A couple." He wanted even more, but he knew he would need Mason to see how it could work, how it could be if they both put in the time. He had almost three weeks for the trial run. As proof.

"I'm in." Mason took a shaky breath. "I'm in. I want you to meet my goddaughter, and Rick and Jefferson. I know it's crazy, but I need you to meet them. And we need to be in Texas close to Sammy's due date. We can't miss that."

"No, we can't. We'll get Maydell and Rachel on the travel schedule." Maydell would love Rachel.

"Rachel's in on this? You've spoken to her?"

"Not really. Just last night. She's a smart cookie, though. She said if she was going to work for me too, she'd have to train someone else to do the event stuff."

"Yes. Absolutely. We can focus too, if we get the chance. Who knows? We'll figure it out."

"We will. After Christmas. Kiss me again? Then we can have breakfast." Noah had never been more pleased with a presentation, or a negotiation, in his whole life.

"I think I can, yes." Mason lifted his face, brought their lips together. "Seal the deal, you know?"

"Much better than a handshake." He kissed his lover deep, wanting Mason to feel everything he felt.

He'd done it. He'd really done it.

Shit and shinola.

Chapter Twenty-Seven

"GREAT party, Mason!" Sammy said, leaning against him. "Seriously. This is perfect."

Mason looked around with a nod. He was pretty damn good at his job, even when he had to work with the poor, unfortunate lady who had been hired to coordinate this party before he had become the exclusive Wright event coordinator.

"Do you need to sit?" He smiled at Sammy, hoping that was sparkling grape juice. It had to be. She was super-duper careful.

"I'm good. I promise. You're as big a worrywart as Noah."

"Yes. You're the most pregnant ever." He winked at her. "Did you get the e-card from Trev and Bryan? They're in Maui."

"I did! I can't wait to see what you're doing with their wedding. Trev says it needs to be delightfully trashy."

"We have some time. They want to do it in September or October, I think."

"Do you ever get tired of it?" she asked.

"What, honey?"

"Organizing other people's weddings?"

Suddenly Noah's hand was on his back. "Don't be a bitch, Sammy. Come dance with me."

Mason chuckled and took Noah's hand. "It's not the first time I've been asked, Mister. It won't be the last."

He had his Noah. Every day. Every night.

No one even blinked when they moved together to the wee dance floor. "Did I just hear you say Trev was in Maui? Wasn't he supposed to help Rachel?"

"She kicked him out after one day. She has a temp for the holidays, and then she'll start interviewing." Mason chuckled, the sound wry. "I told you she wouldn't stand for his bullshit. She's fierce."

Trev was a man in love. Mason got that.

"She is. Maydell wants to adopt her." Noah swung him in a wide circle. "Do you ever get tired of it, honey?"

"What's that, Mister?" The lights were so pretty, making this little ballroom in Texas look like a winter wonderland.

"Making everyone's perfect day perfect?"

Jonah went by on a conga line that totally didn't match the easy swing music, waving like a drunken monkey.

"That's what I do, Noah. There's a joy to it, huh?"

"I know I called Sammy a bitch for asking, but I do wonder sometimes. I'm glad you really love it."

Mr. and Mrs. Wright went by, doing a polka-cha-cha mixture.

He chuckled. "Shut up and dance with me, Mister. This is the best party."

"It is. Someone did a great job. This party planner I know." Noah danced him in a circle, the music changing to a waltz. Something Texas.

"Someone with a certain rustic charm."

"Exactly. I love this song." Noah hummed to him, the dance getting some serious footwork going on. Good thing he knew how to follow.

There was nothing like dancing with the man that you loved. Not a bit.

They ended the song with a flourish, right in front of the little Texas swing band he'd hired on Gene's recommendation. Heck, Noah even dipped him.

Noah's momma had to be swallowing her tongue.

When Noah lifted him back up, there was a smattering of applause, and he laughed, his cheeks hot.

Waving at the band, Noah kept them from starting another song. "Give me a little chingaling, guys."

Mason tried to disengage a little, assuming this was the official "Merry Christmas, y'all" part of the evening. Silly man. This was a little early.

"Thanks." Noah held him fast. "Hey, y'all! Can I get everyone to gather around, please?" Noah gave him a reassuring smile.

The crowd of high-level executives and family came close, Sammy waving at them, a huge smile on her face.

Mason tilted his head. That was his first clue that something was going on here.

"Thank you! I want to thank everyone for coming, and the party is hardly over, but I wanted to share something with my closest friends and family, and this seems like the perfect time. I know everyone has met Mason."

He swore by all he held holy, if Noah announced that they had discovered that sex in the private plane was the most fun ever, Mason was going to pinch him.

Mason just waved and prayed, trying to keep the pleasant smile on his face.

Noah went on. "And I think most of you know how I feel about Mason here. The last few weeks have been the best of my life, and I think both of us are pretty well convinced we're gonna make this dual-city thing work."

He squeezed Noah's hand, his cheeks on fire. Oh God, so sweet.

Noah took a deep breath, just like he did anytime he had something super important to say. Then he turned toward Mason. "Honey, you do the best things for people. Make their happiest days as perfect as you can. I want to give you your perfect day."

Taking his hand, Noah went down on one knee.

"Mister?" The whole world went sparkly, and for a heartbeat, he thought he'd pass out, but there was no way he was missing a second of this. Not one motherfucking second.

Noah nodded, reaching down to tug a little black box out of his pocket. "I know I said I wasn't the marrying kind, honey, but that was just my momma talking."

Momma Wright cackled like a huge bird from about three feet away, making them both jump. "Just ask him, boy."

Opening the ring box, Noah smiled. "Mason, will you marry me?"

He didn't even look at the ring. All he could see was Noah's eyes. "With all my heart, Mr. Wright. With all my heart."

Epilogue

FORD checked the punch bowl that was sitting out under the tent with the food. Anything in mayo was sitting on ice, which Tiny replenished at regular intervals.

June really was the best time for a wedding at the Leanin' N. The weather was perfect, the alpine meadows blooming, and the view was stunning.

"How's it going, Uncle Ford?" Quartz smiled at him, that little yappy dog on one arm, Frank the basset on the other. "They like each other."

"I'd hope so, son. They live on the same ranch half the year."

"With a pit bull and a Great Pyrenees." Quartz shook his head. "That's a lot of dog."

"It's a big ranch, I hear." He pulled a cocktail wiener off the bar of nibbles so he could feed half to each dog. "You doing okay?"

"Yes, sir. I was worried y'all were fixin' to ask me to take care of the baby."

Oh, Lord. He managed not to laugh, but it was a near thing.

"I think his momma has that under control." He glanced over to where Sammy sat in a lounge chair, baby on her shoulder. She looked amazing, her beaming smile taking in all comers.

She raised one hand to him, and he nodded, shot her a smile.

"I'm going to look in on Mr. O'Reilly, kiddo."

"In the kitchen with Daddy and Geoff and Mr. Wright."

"Thank you. You heading for the dog run?"

"Yessir. They need to run." Quartz looked at Frank. "Or waddle."

"Don't let him trip on those ears." He brushed off his jeans and made the familiar path to the kitchen. No matter what they did, this was the heart of this place, so Ford had given in and let it be. People gathered here naturally.

He stepped up, almost running smack into Tiny, who was on his way out. "Sorry, Mr. Ford. They're eating nibbles like crazy out there."

"Keep them fed, man. That's the secret to success." Between Mrs. Wright and the three hooligans Noah had brought in and the two personal assistants, they were enjoying their snacks. That was okay. Nobody dieted at a wedding.

"Hey! Ford, come taste this dip." Geoff scooped up a pile of some kind of hot dip on a tortilla chip for him.

"Whoa, spicy."

Stoney walked by and took a huge bite. "Damn, Geoff. I like that."

Noah nodded, the big Texan looking like he was ten years younger. "I think it needs one more jalapeno."

Texans.

"I think it will burn someone's taste buds off if you do. And I lived in Santa Fe." Ford scowled.

Noah raised a brow. "Wuss."

Mason started laughing, the sound low and merry. "Listen to you. You'd think I was back in Dallas."

"Cowboys are the same all over," Geoff said. "I think I'll make one more pan and make it hotter. That way we have a choice."

"Works for me." Mason went back to making rainbow-colored bows for God knew what. He also had little cardboard tags that read "Mr. and Mr."

"Aren't you supposed to be letting someone else do that, honey?" Noah shook his head, the smile so fond. "Rach has Benji, right? He's the most rainbow person I know."

"Benji is at a Chamber of Commerce luncheon today, handing out business cards and lead chasing. He'll come up tonight."

Benji was Mason's new assistant, and he was the polar opposite of the much-teased Trevor. Sweet, quiet, given to argyle and mustard-colored socks.

"Mason, love?"

Mason looked up at Noah, who was smiling.

"I need you. Come on."

Like magic, Mason stood up, took Noah's hand, and Noah waved the other hand. "Someone take care of this?"

Stoney chuckled softly. "No problem, Mr. Wright. We got this."

"Thanks." Noah tugged Mason away, their laughter trailing behind them.

Ford winked at Stoney. "How come that doesn't work for me?"

"Because you have to preface it with 'nice boots.'"

"Now you tell me." He leaned down, kissed his husband in that sweet, hot spot right beneath his ear. "Tonight, lover. I've got your number."

"You do. For now, though, you need to sit with me and make bows." Stoney poured them both a cup of coffee. "I mean, Mason found his Mr. Wright. We have to make his day perfect."

Coming in October 2017

REAMSPUN DESIRES

Dreamspun Desires #43
The Bunny and the Billionaire by Louisa Masters

Spending their fortunes and losing their hearts.

Hardworking Australian nurse Ben Adams inherits a substantial sum and decides to tour Europe. In Monaco, the home of glamour and the idle rich, he meets French billionaire playboy Léo Artois. After getting off on the wrong foot—as happens when one accuses a stranger of being part of the Albanian mafia—their attraction blazes. Léo, born to the top tier of society, has never known limits, and Ben, used to budgeting every cent, finds it difficult to adjust to not only Léo's world, but also the changes wealth brings to his own life.

As they make allowances for each other's foibles, Ben slowly appreciates the finer things, and Léo widens his perspective. They both know one thing: this is not a typical holiday romance, and they're not ready to say goodbye.

Dreamspun Desires #44
The Fireman's Pole by Sue Brown

It's springtime in Calminster village, but things are already heating up. Sexy fireman Dale Maloney is new to the local station, and when Dale backs the company fire truck into the village maypole, he attracts the ire—and attention—of Lord Edwin Calminster. Soon after meeting Dale, Edwin breaks off his relationship with his girlfriend, and the sparks between them are quickly fanned into flames.

Unfortunately the passion between Dale and Edwin isn't the only blaze in the village. An arsonist's crimes are escalating, and it's up to Dale and his crew to stop him. As they investigate, an unscrupulous business partner attempts to coerce Edwin into marrying his daughter. The mayday parade is around the corner, but they have plenty of fires to put out before Edwin can finally slide down the fireman's pole.

#39

The Teddy Bear Club by Sean Michael

The Teddy Bear Club

Two lonely men. One perfect family.

Aiden Lake adopted his institutionalized sister's two daughters, and he's a good dad. He works nights on websites and gets in his adult time twice a week at the Roasty Bean, where he meets with other single gay parents.

Devon Smithson wants to be a good dad now that his sixteen-year-old sister asked him to babysit her newborn… three months ago. But he's overwhelmed with the colicky baby. An invitation to the daddy-and-kid gatherings at the café is a godsend. The pot is sweetened when his friendship with Aiden develops into more—maybe even something that can last.

But the mother who kicked Dev out for being gay wants to get her claws into the baby, and she doesn't care if she tears Dev, Aiden, and everything they're building apart in the process.

#40

Out of the Shadows by K.C. Wells

Can he step out of the shadows and into love's light?

Eight years ago, Christian Hernandez moved to Jamaica Plain in southern Boston, took refuge in his apartment, and cut himself off from the outside world. And that's how he'd like it to stay.

Josh Wendell has heard his coworkers gossip about the occupant of apartment #1. No one sees the mystery man, and Josh loves a mystery. So when he is hired to refurbish the apartment's kitchen and bathrooms, Josh is eager to discover the truth behind the rumors.

When he comes face-to-face with Christian, Josh understands why Christian hides from prying eyes. As the two men bond, Josh sees past his exterior to the man within, and he likes what he sees. But can Christian find the courage to emerge from the darkness of his lonely existence for the man who has claimed his heart?